ZAKOLOR

NACUSTI CHRONICLES VOLUME I

J. R. DOUGLAS

· Firepost Press ·

For my parents, who raised a Dreamer.

WASTELANDS
Pywell Mountains
Merinthia's Pass
DARLANGSON
Anguis River
NALAWIN
REPUBLIC OF EVARTIA
Janlaka
Masdaan
Karanadee River
REGADENSIA
WESLINTON
Tor'alan
Gort'haal
Lindomer
VALECIUM
SOUTHERN ISLES
Bernadooth
Densba

CONTENTS

Chapter 1

THE BEGINNING

Zakolor didn't know why he was running, but his legs pumped with fury, carrying him swiftly through a wooded region. It was dark and he wasn't safe. Thick pines swayed and croaked with heavy gusts of wind. If he had the time to slow down and look around, he may have been reminded of the area near his hometown of Densba. But he didn't—couldn't—stop running. A looming presence shadowed his every step as he struggled to see through the blanket of darkness on the moonless night.

Ragged breath pushed in and out of his chest. How long had he kept the pace? He didn't know, but he needed to stay ahead of the unnerving being. A flicker of movement to his right spurred him on to even greater speed. Whatever was chasing him was gaining ground, almost on top of him. Stealing a glance backward he saw nothing, but a low-hanging branch clipped his shoulder and forced him to the ground. He rolled over, trembling with fear as the darkness swallowed him.

Then it was over.

"Zakolor. Zakolor! Pay attention!" His teacher's stern voice cut above the laughter of his classmates.

"Sorry, Ms. Miranda." He winced. It happened again; he was daydreaming about his recurring nightmare. Could it be a nightmare if it haunted him during the day as well? He wiped the sweat from his brow and sunk lower in his chair, trying to disappear.

Ms. Miranda wouldn't allow that.

"Now that we have your attention, Mr. Keldin, I was hoping you could describe the details of The Contract to us." Ms. Miranda had a way of turning questions into orders.

Zak huffed. *I'm not a child*, he thought. He was seventeen, an adult by all standards. Only a few more months and he'd be done with the tiny, dilapidated schoolhouse. Then he could finally work with his father at the smithy.

"Right, The Contract," he said, knowing he was trapped and at Ms. Miranda's mercy. "It's the agreement the gods signed after the war."

"Which war?" she countered.

He grabbed at the jade pendant hanging around his neck, running his thumb over the surface. "The...um..." He looked around the room as if the answer would manifest on the ceiling or out the window. Luckily, his friend Kalbick had a tendency to scribble the answer to every question Ms. Miranda asked in his notes. He slid the parchment over just enough for Zak to peek at it without being caught. "The...Guardian War," he said, trying to disguise his sideways reading.

Ms. Miranda's eyes narrowed, staring suspiciously at Zak for a moment. "Very good," she said, apparently satisfied if not slightly surprised. "Now, as we all know, the gods once ruled over all living things. They were cruel and controlling, deciding the course of the world on a whim. We refer to this as the Era of Dominion. They created the Guardians to guide all creatures and solidify their presence in the physical plane. Guardians took many different shapes and sizes, and were bound to their altars."

Sandra-May's hand shot into the air, rippling her stringy red hair with the movement. Without waiting to be called on, she immediately started asking her question. "How did the Guardians end up on our side?"

"A fine question, Sandra-May. Does anyone know?"

Kal hunched over his desk, furiously scribbling the answer as his blond hair slowly fell to hang by his eyes. The rest of the class remained silent.

"No one?" Ms. Miranda waited another moment. "Very well. The Guardians recognized the suffering the gods brought to us. When man and elf banded together in opposition to the gods, the Guardians offered their aid. By sacrificing themselves, the Guardians infused their powers with six worthy mages—three men and three elves—and thus created the *Nacusti*."

"What happened to the Guardians? Did any survive the war?" Sandra-May asked. She didn't bother raising her hand this time.

"No one knows. Their altars appear to be abandoned, though some claim their presence can be felt. Two of the six *Nacusti* survived the war, the elf Temaway Galeria and man Adrastus Belcour. With their triumph over the gods, they drafted The Contract, a magical document that limited the power of the gods and granted us true autonomy over our lives for the first time."

The bell in the village center sounded, marking the end of the school day. "Alright, class. That's it for today. We'll pick back up with the three gods and their rotating throne of power tomorrow."

Zak let out a long sigh as he gathered his things. He had daydreamed through half the lesson. *Another day wasted,* he thought.

"Here," Kal said. He held out his notes with the scribbled answers. He even filled in the questions so Zak would know what they were answering. "You looked a bit distracted again today."

"You're brilliant." Zak gave his friend a thankful grin. Kal always looked after Zak, even with something as small as studying for a test. "It's that dream, I can't stop thinking about it. Not to mention the smell in here could daze a horse."

"Excuses," Kal teased with a roll of his eyes.

As they left the schoolhouse, the village of Densba opened into a semi-circular clearing with rows of buildings standing defiantly against the surrounding forest. Nearly every structure had an affliction: the inn was missing shingles (particularly obvious on a damp night), the council building had a door that didn't sit on the hinges quite right, and more than a few houses boasted crooked, creaking porches.

Deep into the countryside on the small southern island, the Densbanians were hard-working people to whom luxury was foreign. The current war between the Consortium and the League of Kingdoms didn't help matters either. Any extra resources and time that could be spared were sent to the League. Despite the lack of luster, the country folk were proud of their dwellings, their town, and each other.

Almost everyone lived in town except a few farmers who preferred to stay closer to their fields. Zak's and Kal's houses sat at the end of the semi-circle of buildings with a forge wedged between them, shared by their fathers. Zak and Kal trained as apprentices for years, studying the craft of their fathers, and their fathers before them. Their families, while not related, had close ties that reached back generations to the initial settling of the Southern Isles.

As they walked toward their homes, Zak heard a single yell behind him, then a few more sounded off. He turned and saw several people standing in the village center, pointing to something in the sky, shielding their eyes from the late afternoon sun.

Zak looked skyward too, squinting to see what caused the commotion. There was a small, black dot. It was far away but moving fast toward Densba.

"What is that?" Kal asked.

"There's at least one answer you don't have." He elbowed Kal, drawing a smile from him. "C'mon, let's go find out."

When they reached the village center a sizeable crowd had formed, something that only happened on the Year Festival or for the occasional brawl at the inn. The small dot grew larger, and soon Zak saw beating wings on what appeared to be a man.

"Is that a Magerus?" a voice asked from the crowd.

"Impossible!" said another.

"Well look! It's a flying man! What else could it be?"

"What would a Magerus want here of all places?"

Zak's heartbeat quickened. *Could it be possible? Could a Magerus be here?* His palms were slick with sweat as he clutched his jade pendant. He and Kal exchanged a confused and excited look. Nothing *ever* happened in Densba.

Several more minutes of disbelief and muttered remarks passed until the winged man arrived. Zak shielded his eyes as the wind from his strong wings buffeted the group with dirt and debris. The man gracefully set both feet on the ground and the Densbanians circled about him as his enormous, hawk-like wings glittered gold and faded away as if they never existed. The group let out a low rumble of awe at the display.

Zak couldn't help but be equally amazed. In their small village, few people possessed magic, and when they did it was used for farming or small tricks to entertain at the inn.

This man was different. He had real magic, real power.

At the back of the gathering, Zak could hardly see anything. "Let's get closer," he suggested to Kal. They snaked between bodies to the front of the group to get a better look at the newcomer.

He was tall, well over six feet, Zak guessed, with brownish-gold hair that was cropped short. His clothes were shiny and smooth, a matching tunic and dark brown breeches, a beige robe with white trim, leather boots, and a jeweled belt with an evenly adorned and magnificent sword.

"Hello, everyone. I am Sorwin, High Magus and Second Prince to the Kingdom of Darlangson. I will be your scout this year."

As he spoke, the crowd stared at him and cherished every word, every second of his presence. A magerus and a royal? It was almost too much for the small crowd to digest as they broke into excited chatter. As the initial awe subsided, questions began flying.

"Where's Fenton? He's the normal scout," asked a man to Zak's right, his hands covered in soil from working the fields.

"Fenton has been temporarily reassigned to another village," Sorwin said.

"Why is a High Magus scouting?" Kal asked.

Zak's attention snapped to his friend, shocked by his audacity. He swore Kal's never-ending quest for knowledge would get him into trouble someday.

Sorwin smiled. "I believe that's a matter to discuss with your council leader. Are they present? I would share words, if so." He continued smiling through the barrage of questions. He did say he was a royal, so Zak guessed a few questions from bewildered villagers would do little to shake his composure.

A stout, burly man pushed forward through the crowd. Normally Zak considered Joryl rather imposing, but he paled next to the greatness of Sorwin. It wasn't only the clothes and finery that set them apart, but the way Sorwin held his chin slightly up with his shoulders back, as if he waited for someone or something to impress him. Joryl, on the other hand, leaned forward as he walked and looked as if he would be very comfortable in a tavern with sticky floors and stale bread. Yet Zak knew the council leader had a fierce kindness in him, despite appearances.

"Now, now, everyone," Joryl said. "Calm down, calm down. We should be so lucky to have one of the five Mageri in the world here in our village!" He nodded to Sorwin with awkward deference before continuing. "As you all know, the League of Kingdoms sends a scout to us between Summerfall and Autumnrise every year. And every year our youths line up for evaluation to see if they can aid the war effort. It is a great honor being selected for service, and I'm sure the League has its reasons for sending him—um, the Magerus."

Joryl turned to Sorwin. "I am Joryl, the council leader," he said shakily. "Anything you need at all, please don't wait to ask, Sir, um, Mage Sir, your, uh, Greatness, Sir." A few scattered snickers rolled through the crowd. The need for titles and formalities was an uncommon occurrence in Densba.

Sorwin dipped his head in acknowledgment. "I merely require a place to stay and your company for a few minutes, Council Leader. And please, call me Sorwin. I'm not very fond of titles, though I'm required to state them at my arrival." He still wore a charming smile as the two men walked toward the inn, the crowd parting around them as they went. As soon as they were out of earshot, conversation erupted and caught like wildfire.

"Three Fires!" Kal shouted. "A High Magus—here! Can you believe it, Zak? I can't wait to pick his brain about becoming a mage. I think I might join the League this year."

"Yeah, it's really something," Zak said. *But why is he here?*

Mageri traveled for their personal agendas; they were rare and powerful enough to more or less do whatever they wanted. But they never traveled somewhere as remote as the southern islands, and never to scout. Scouting wasn't difficult. Common mages with little talent who came a copper a dozen could handle the assignment with ease.

"We should get home, our parents will wonder where we are," Zak said. Kal nodded and continued spouting rhetorical questions and excited statements as they walked home for the second time that day.

For some reason, Sorwin's arrival put Zak on edge. He was having difficulty shaking his apprehension, though he desperately wanted to. Kal had been identified as a high-potential soldier and mage years ago. Zak wasn't sure why his friend declined the offer of recruitment year after year, and when pressed for answers he always shrugged off the question and changed the subject. If Zak was offered recruitment—which he never was—he would have joined without a moment's hesitation. He wanted to travel, to experience the world, to learn magic. He secretly wanted much more than to be a blacksmith, but what was the point of sharing those aspirations when he knew they were just wishes and dreams?

Zak parted ways with Kal once they reached their homes on either side of the shared forge. When he stepped through the front door it was almost suppertime and his mother was scrubbing the floor while soup bubbled over the fire. She glanced up as Zak entered.

"Well, if it isn't our little adventurer. Your father is in a mood," she said.

Zak silently cursed himself. He and Kal were supposed to hurry home immediately after lessons to help at the forge with a large order.

"Sorry, Ma. The scout came today and we got a bit distracted," he said.

"Don't apologize to me, it's him you'll need to be dealin' with."

At that moment his father stomped into the house, crossed to the hearth and smelled the soup, then sat down at the table in the middle of the room, not once looking at his son.

Zak knew he had disappointed his father. He didn't move, fear and shame fusing him to the floor until his mother beckoned him over to the table for supper. They ate in silence, his father's eyes never leaving his bowl. Zak stole a glance every so often but didn't dare look for too long. Hopefully, once he explained why he was late his father would understand. All Zak needed was the courage to speak.

His mother broke the silence for him. "So, how is Fenton this year? Does he still have that old mule?" she asked.

"Actually, Fenton didn't come this year," Zak said.

"Oh really? That's too bad. I always enjoyed talking with him about junipers. That man has the greenest thumb I've ever seen. Who did they send this year?"

"The High Magus Sorwin Darlangson." Zak blurted it out, almost too fast for comprehension. His eyes darted between his parents, waiting for a reaction. They both froze, spoons hovering in midair spilling soup back into their bowls. They held each other's gaze for a long time and, once they regained their composure, looked at Zak.

"Are you sure? You couldn't be mistaken, could you?"

His mother sounded almost desperate, her tone pleading.

He was hoping they would be curious, impressed, or maybe even have a lackluster reaction. If they felt Sorwin's presence was insignificant, maybe his nerves would calm and he'd be reassured he was overreacting. Instead, they were skeptical too. Their reactions made him more worried.

"That's who he claimed to be. And he had wings, so I don't think he *could* be lying."

Another look was shared between his parents. "Are you alright?" Zak asked them. He rocked uneasily in his chair.

"How have you been sleeping lately?" his mother asked, ignoring his question.

"Fine," he said, "a few nightmares but nothing that serious."

Again his parents looked even more worried.

"What's going on?" He was becoming annoyed at this point. Why were they behaving so strangely?

"Tell the boy, Clairise," Zak's father said. "We should have done it years ago anyway."

"Ageric!" Clairise shot an angry look at him across the table. Zak's attention shifted back and forth between his parents, confused and irritated.

"Tell me what?" he asked.

His mother inhaled and exhaled deeply. "You weren't born to us, Zakolor." Her voice was soft, little more than a whisper.

Zak stared at both of his parents, not quite sure what to make of the unexpected revelation.

"What do you mean? Is this a joke?" They were both

silent. "I...I'm not yours?" His mind raced almost as fast as his heartbeat thundering in his chest. How had talking about a scout led to this?

"Oh, of course you're ours!" Clairise reached, wrapping both of her warm hands around his sweaty ones. "Please, never think otherwise. Your father and I...Cerevita didn't bless us with children in the common way, but we knew we wanted a family. We went north to the orphanage in Bernadooth to find our child. But the youngest they had was over a decade, and pardon me for being selfish but I wanted a baby to raise as my own!" The last part came out as a sob with a rush of tears. Ageric placed a supportive hand on her shoulder and stared at Zakolor, his expression unreadable.

Clairise continued. "After that we returned to the inn and packed our things, thinking our dreams dashed. On our way out of town, a strange man stopped us and asked if we were still interested in adopting a baby. Your father and I were startled that he knew our intentions because we only spoke with the people at the orphanage, and he obviously wasn't one of them. But then he pulled a baby, you, from the folds of his cloak and I just knew, I *knew* Cerevita had a plan for us after all. He told us to take you, that no payment was necessary, that all we had to do was not tell a soul where we found you." Her crying had stopped for the moment and she dabbed at her tears with a cloth napkin. She took a deep breath and resumed her story.

"So there we were, standing in the middle of the road, very confused but very thankful, with you in our arms. We did exactly as the man said and left. A few weeks after getting home you began having fits."

"Fits?" Zak asked. They never told him that before, either.

"Oh yes. One moment you would be sound asleep, and then the next you would be crying so hard you coughed yourself into a fit. I felt terrible, but I could do little except try and comfort you. I didn't know what was wrong. A few days after the fits started the man appeared on our doorstep." She said this last part more seriously, a darkness crossing her face. The change in her demeanor scared Zak.

"He asked us what happened to you and if you were hurt in some way. I was outraged at his implications and we nearly tossed him out, but he only asked if he could see you. We let him, figured we owed him that much anyway. And he saw you were hale and whole."

"Who was he?" Zak asked.

Clairise shook her head. "We asked who he was and where you came from, but he answered nothing. Just as he was leaving he gave us the jade necklace you're wearing."

At the mention of his necklace, Zak realized he had been running his thumb across it for so long his finger had gone numb. He stopped and scrunched his brow, looking at his mother. She answered his unasked question.

"He told us to put it on you and that you should never take it off for any reason whatsoever. He never told us why, but that your life depended on it."

Zak looked down at his necklace. Not once in his life had the thought of removing it crossed his mind. He leaned back in his chair, overwhelmed and thoroughly frustrated. Clairise and Ageric. They weren't his natural parents.

"Why didn't you tell me sooner? That I'm not yours." It came out sharper than he intended, but he needed to know.

"But you *are* ours. You were given to us, and I thank Mother Cerevita every day that she blessed us with you," Clairise said. "We didn't tell you because there wasn't much to tell. Your history and family aren't known to us, and the man requested we keep your beginnings a secret. We thought it best if you didn't have to keep it too."

Zak wasn't satisfied. Far from it. Who was his natural family? Who was the man that gave him away? Why did he have to wear the jade? Why were his parents afraid at the mention of Sorwin? That didn't make sense; Sorwin's arrival started them down this path of revelation. Was there a connection between the magerus and his history? He had a hundred questions and no information that remotely resembled an answer. When he didn't speak, Clairise continued.

"The man also said that if any League official besides the normal scout came here we should leave quickly and quietly. We assumed you must be important to them somehow."

"How? I get tested every year and Fenton always says I'd be an average soldier without a speck of magic." Zak knew he sounded childish but he didn't care. Too many emotions were swirling inside him to mind his manners.

"We're staying here," Ageric said, breaking his silence.

"But Ageric, the man said—" Clairise started.

"I know what he said." He raised his voice slightly. "From his reputation, the High Magus Sorwin seems noble enough. I don't think we have to go running off just yet. And where would we go? Bernadooth? There are greater evils in that city than a League official. We're staying here for now. Avoid the mage, Zakolor. I don't want you to get tested this year."

Zak started to argue. "But what if I have magic this year?" He'd never demonstrated a gift before, but he still tried every year to see if anything changed. Most people showed signs of magic early in life. It was rare—but not impossible—to develop magic where there was no sign of it before. So he held out hope that maybe he still had a chance to live his adventurous dreams. "I could be recruited, then the League would send you payment and—"

"No. You will stay away from him," Ageric said firmly.

Zak fumed, growling in frustration and jumping up from the table, running outside. Clairise called his name and followed him, but he heard Ageric stop her in the yard.

"He needs some time, Clairi."

Zak ran aimlessly, feet pounding into the earth, not thinking where he was going. None of this was fair. Questions, fears, and limitations piled on top of him. All he wanted to do was escape. He wished desperately to be gifted so he could leave Densba, go to the mainland, join the war effort, and make a difference in the world. He'd settle for something far less grand too, wishing for a small amount of control over his life.

He slowed his pace and looked at his surroundings. A river that ran right outside the town fed a waterfall that fell into a beautiful valley with a small pond lined with thick rows of trees. Standing at the rim of the cliff, listening to the rumble of water pouring down its side, watching it turn to glittery mist as it crashed to the bottom...it reminded him of something, but he wasn't sure what. There was a memory he couldn't quite recall, dancing at the edge of his thoughts.

The wind blew, ruffling his hair and clothes. Zak closed his eyes and spread his arms wide, letting the breeze pass through him unhindered.

As he stood there, he thought he heard something. Voices? He strained to listen. It was difficult; they passed by so quickly, whispering and flitting about as if they rode the wind. One of the voices came close, shouting in his ear. The sudden loud noise jolted Zak out of his trance. He blinked several times and shook his head, scolding himself for letting his imagination run away again. Whoever heard of voices on the wind?

He started walking home—slowly—thinking about the events of the day. The irritated, helpless feeling crept up again. He felt lost, unsure what he should do about any of it, or if he could do anything at all.

There was one thing Zak did know: he wanted to be tested by Sorwin. He couldn't shake the feeling that this year was different, that Sorwin was here for a reason besides scouting. Zak resolved in that moment that he wanted to find out about his past, even if it meant disobeying his father.

CHAPTER 2
EVALUATION

The next morning Sorwin noticed the village still buzzed over his arrival. A magerus was extremely overqualified for scouting, let alone in faraway Densba. The people, however, threw their suspicions aside—or at least kept them held close. In Sorwin's presence, their fears and doubts receded in the glow of his confidence, competence, and kindness.

A few gifts were left outside his door, appearing at some point during the night. When he breakfasted at the inn, a few villagers greeted him with bows and awkward honorifics. They didn't seem to know what to do with him, but it was obvious they didn't want to mistreat him.

Sorwin found the almost worship-like attention endearing and slightly humorous as he left the inn and walked along the road to an open field outside of town. While the villagers might envy his power, wealth, and stature, he envied them at least twice as much. He had often visited a town very similar to this in his youth. Accipia, it was named. Sitting on the open plains of the Western Expanse, he learned to work fields, tend sheep and cow, raise barns and repair doors and windows. He enjoyed the simplicity, the directness of making something with his hands. Somehow he always felt happier, warmer on the plains of Accipia than he ever had in his family's castle, nestled in the soaring Darlangson peaks. His namesake.

The Darlangson creed upheld that perspective and empathy were paramount; that a ruler must understand who and what they would rule. So, Sorwin worked alongside the villagers, learned their way of life, what made them happy and sad. He loved Accipia dearly, and the villagers loved him even more for his sincere devotion to their well-being. It had been seven long years since he visited Accipia. Every day he longed to return.

He knew he couldn't, that it was an impossible desire. The League of Kingdom's ruling council was comprised of nine magical officials, several military leaders and private benefactors, and the rulers from the four kingdoms: Darlangson, Regadensia, The Republic of Evartia, and Weslinton. Being a magerus and a noble, Sorwin was part of the League's ruling council and therefore bound to the capital city, Tor'alan.

With a heavy sigh he continued on his path toward the field outside of town, shaking his daydreams away. *This is why I volunteer for faraway journeys*, he reminded himself. *To escape from the incessant rancor that thrives in cities, especially Tor'alan*. Even a temporary reprieve was a welcome one.

He had enjoyed his morning among the people of Densba, but with the village bell ringing in the afternoon, his assignment—his search—would begin.

"Hello, everyone!" A smile spread across his face as he

greeted a large group of boys and girls assembled in the field, ages ranging roughly from ten to eighteen. Some of them snapped to attention, while a few of the younger ones looked visibly afraid, trembling and ducking behind their larger fellows. *We'll start slow, then.* "First, let's get you sorted into pairs."

Sorwin assessed the crowd and quickly separated them by size and weight. As he divided his students, he spoke to prepare them for what lay ahead. "The next few days could prove to be pivotal in your life if we determine you have talent to serve the League. I know most families have mixed feelings about scouting. If offered recruitment, you have the opportunity to bring not only honor to your family, but also compensation for your valiant efforts. However, accepting recruitment also means several years away from home and accepting the risks of war. I say this not to scare you, but to ensure you realize to the fullest extent what it is you volunteer for.

"To receive an offer from the League, you must prove to be physically capable, magically gifted, or, for those rare few, to be talented in both." Sorwin stepped back and admired his work with a nod.

"Now that you're all sorted, we will begin with the physical test. Pay attention, now, and learn these basic attacks and defensive maneuvers." Sorwin adopted a wide stance and the children mimicked him with a seriousness and intensity beyond their years on their faces.

"Come on! We're late!" Kal hissed.

The scouting session had already started in the field ahead.

"Coming!" Zak half walked, half jogged nervously behind Kal. "I think I am. Maybe. I don't know if I should."

Last night he was determined to meet Sorwin, but the closer he drew to the field the more uneasy he became. What if his parents really did know what was best for him? But they weren't his natural parents. Maybe he should see if Sorwin knew anything. But was that too risky?

Before he made a decision, he had walked right into the middle of the scouting session. The rest of the kids stared at him as he stood there, lost in thought.

"Will you be joining us today?" asked a kind voice from Zak's left. He turned and saw Sorwin smiling at him.

Zak nodded sheepishly.

"Wonderful! Would you join with that pair of boys there? We're practicing our technique in hand-to-hand combat."

"Looks like you made up your mind, whether you meant to or not," Kal said, grabbing Zak's shirt and pulling him to the back near the boys Sorwin mentioned.

The Magerus continued leading them through simple offensive and defensive maneuvers, showing them how to punch, kick, and block. This was the same as when Fenton scouted. Many of the older kids were already familiar with the movements, having practiced them each year—and often throughout the year, for those that dreamed of joining the League. After a half hour of the repetitive motions, Sorwin turned them loose on their partners to test their skills.

Zak squared off against Brandon, a boy with short dust-colored hair. They approached one another with a wariness.

"Good luck, then," Zak said. Brandon was the son of the butcher and the same age as Zak. Densba was a small town and they knew of each other, but they never really spoke.

"Yeah, you too," Brandon said.

Zak was cautious and hesitant, waiting for Brandon to take the initiative. He did, rushing at Zak with a right hook. Zak barely got his forearm up to block the attack. *He's fast!* Zak thought.

With their arms locked above their heads, Brandon kicked with his left leg and connected solidly with Zak's hip. He fell, landing hard on the unforgiving ground.

Brandon smirked at his victory. taking a few steps back to give Zak room to regain his footing.

As Zak stood, he brushed the dirt from his clothes and felt his hip tenderly. Brandon hadn't held back one bit. With newfound respect, Zak watched carefully for any twitch of movement that might precede the next attack.

Brandon came in again, leading with his left fist this time. Zak blocked with his arm and grabbed Brandon's wrist as he launched an uppercut with his other fist. They stood locked together for many seconds before Zak managed to throw Brandon's left arm wide and brought his knee up hard into his opponent's stomach. Brandon lurched and fell backward.

He sat, coughing and catching his breath for a few moments before attempting to stand again.

It was Zak's turn to smirk, though only for a moment. He wiped the smile from his face and reminded himself to focus. He wasn't entirely sure he should be here, but now that he was he wanted to make the most of it.

While he waited for Brandon to recover, Zak looked around the field. Nearly all of the other miniature battles were progressing the same way as his: each partner taking a hit and then dealing a blow in return.

Some matches, however, were more one-sided, such as the one Kal fought. He dominated his opponent, a stout black-haired boy who lived not far from this field. Kal flitted around the boy, using his superior speed and reach to strike repeatedly before the boy could even consider blocking.

Sorwin walked around the field, monitoring the battles. Zak's stomach swirled as he watched the mage, maybe from excitement or nerves or both. Brandon found his feet and assumed a battle stance. Zak refocused his attention as they continued to spar.

The battles continued for another hour before Sorwin called for a halt. At his request, all twenty-four of his students formed a single line. He spent a few moments with each one, praising them for small victories, offering advice on improving technique, and healing any acquired bumps and bruises. Eventually it was Zak's turn.

"You did well. I'm glad you decided to join us," Sorwin said, stopping in front of Zak.

"Thanks." He looked down at his feet, too nervous to

make eye contact. His resolve still abandoned him, perhaps waning with the initial shock of yesterday's events.

"I don't believe I caught your name."

"I'm Zakolor, sir."

"Ah, Zakolor. A fine name. Northern, I believe? Rare to find that in the Southern Isles."

Zak held his breath and continued looking down. He could feel his cheeks warming from nervous energy. How could a name betray so much information about him?

"Thanks," he said again. If he couldn't diversify his responses soon, he may convince Sorwin he was dull, dumb, or both. Maybe that wouldn't be the worst thing; it would almost certainly prevent an offer of recruitment.

"Have you any injuries that need healing?" Sorwin asked.

"Um, yes. My hip and my arm, just there."

Sorwin's hands hovered momentarily over the areas he indicated. They glowed a soft orange and Zak felt the cool sensation of the healing magic. He had never been healed before, but Kal had been once. After starting to help with small jobs in the smithy, Kal severely burned his arm and had to go to Bernadooth for treatment. He said it felt like a cool, concentrated breeze, like if you could wrap the wind around yourself.

As Sorwin finished healing Zak's bruises, a small shock zapped between them. The mage recoiled, rubbing his hand and narrowing his eyes.

Zak had jumped at the shock but stared straight ahead and pretended not to notice. *What in the name of Cerevita was that?*

Sorwin squinted, looking at where the wounds had been and then at Zak. He said nothing for several moments, and finally, Zak had to break the silence.

"Is something the matter?" he asked the mage. He couldn't believe he found his voice.

"No, I don't believe so," Sorwin answered slowly. His eyes continued to dart, evaluating Zak and eventually settled on his jade. "That's an interesting necklace you have. Where did you get it?"

Zak's heart thumped so hard he thought it would leap from his chest. "I—I'm not sure. It was a present a while ago," he lied.

"Hmm." Sorwin moved on to the next student in line.

Zak was too afraid to move. Too afraid to think, breathe, or do anything. Kal walked up next to him.

"I saw you today. You did loads better than last year. Have you been practicing?" He nonchalantly patted Zak on the back, and the physical contact broke him from his stupor.

"He knows!" He whispered loudly, pulling Kal away from the rest of the group.

"Who knows what?"

"Sorwin!" Earlier that morning, Zak had told Kal everything that had happened the night before. "He knows my name is Northern—I didn't even know that—and he was asking questions about my necklace. I think it zapped him!" He should have listened to his parents. Being scouted was a huge mistake.

"Alright, calm down. He's a High Magus, which means he's educated. It's not surprising he knew the origins of your name. And your parents said the jade had magic, right? Didn't it calm your fits or something? Maybe his magic interacted poorly with the jade's. It probably just surprised him."

Kal was very logical and reasonable, which Zak usually appreciated. But right now he needed a friend to worry with him.

"I don't think that's it. He looked suspicious, like I did something wrong. I need to leave before he decides to ask more questions." Zak started walking away on legs that wobbled from exhaustion and anxiety.

"Wait!" Kal grabbed his arm and turned him back around. "If you leave in the middle of scouting he might be more suspicious. I think you should stay for the magical exam."

"What?" Zak couldn't believe what he was hearing.

"I've been thinking about it since Sorwin arrived. Why would a magerus be here? He's obviously looking for something, and what are mageri most interested in looking for? Magic. No offense, but you haven't shown a lick of magic in all the years you've been scouted. Maybe if you show him you have no magic he'll lose interest."

He knew Kal was looking out for him, but hearing his friend's cold evaluation of his abilities still stung.

"Fine," Zak said. He was too anxious to be too offended.

"Right, now that everyone's healed, let's get you back in line. We'll test your magic next," Sorwin said, corralling his students into formation.

Zak looked at Kal, a last surge of fear prodding him to leave. Kal grabbed hold of Zak's shoulders and walked him toward the front of the line. "Just get it over with."

"Kal!" Zak whispered harshly. His feet scuffled on the ground as he tried to push back against his friend. It was the only reaction he mustered before they stopped moving, and he realized he was third in line behind Brandon and Sandra-May.

"Looks like you're first," Sorwin said to Sandra-May. Her hands clasped behind her back as she beamed up at him, apparently overjoyed at having his full attention. Zak couldn't help but roll his eyes. She was always trying to impress the nearest adult.

"What's the test this year?" Sandra-May asked. "Animation? Conjuring? Fenton always had us make flowers talk, or march around the field. I almost had it last year," she said, with not a small degree of self-importance.

"Still didn't get you recruited," Brandon said, half under his breath.

"Shut it!" She whipped around to face him.

"That's enough," Sorwin said with a steady voice. "We're keeping it much simpler this year." He held out his hand. "If you could, using only your thoughts and gestures, move this stone from my palm."

"That's it?" Sandra-May asked, her tone disappointed.

"That's it," Sorwin said, smiling and apparently oblivious to Sandra-May's feelings.

The girl scrunched her nose and focused on the stone. She slowly raised her hand, and the stone followed, slowly and shakily rising. Everyone was silent as it floated, suspended nearly a foot in the air above where it started. After several moments she lowered her hand gently, and the stone lowered softly into Sorwin's palm.

"There, nothing to it," she said. Several beads of sweat dotted Sandra-May's forehead as she exhaled.

"Well done! An effort to be proud of. Who's next?"

"I am." Brandon stepped forward. He concentrated on the stone much like Sandra-May had, but his gesture was different. Instead of slowly raising his arm, he thrust it up into the air in one swift motion, perhaps trying to force the stone to move quicker or further. It did little more than wiggle helplessly like a robin egg just before hatching.

"Hmm. You have some magic. Perhaps another year to develop your connection to it," Sorwin said. Brandon slouched in defeat and stepped aside. "Next?"

Zak's stomach dropped, twisted and burned all at once. It felt like the time he ate old stew, and was sick for days.

Kal gave him a little nudge forward for encouragement. Several of the others began snickering. They knew this was a waste of time. Zak returned to the scouting sessions every year only to be turned away, being declared an average fighter with no magical talents whatsoever.

"Quiet down now, everyone," Sorwin said. "We treat each other with the respect we wish to be shown. Zakolor, wasn't it?"

As Zak stepped forward the group fell silent. "Yes sir." Tension gripped his throat. He wanted to get this over with so he could run home and never disobey his parents again.

"Off you go then," Sorwin said, holding out the stone in his palm.

Zak gave an honest effort, but he wasn't surprised by the results. He focused on the stone and raised his hand slowly and purposefully like Sandra-May had, silently commanding the stone to move. It sat in the mage's hand, staying obstinately motionless.

When nothing happened, Zak dropped his hand and turned to walk away.

"Wait," Sorwin said. Zak turned back, and Sorwin's face creased with confusion as his eyes settled on Zak's jade again. "Would you remove your necklace and try again?"

"I..." Zak didn't have a response. He couldn't remember a time he wasn't wearing it. He looked nervously at Sorwin, then back to Kal. His friend nodded and gestured to do it, confident in his theory Zak would be safe once he proved he had no magic.

"Okay," Zak agreed hesitantly.

He lifted the wrapped leather band from around his neck. Removing the necklace was such a foreign feeling he was confident he had never taken it off. It felt wrong, like he was betraying someone. His knuckles turned white as he held it tight in his fists.

"Breathe easy and steady," Sorwin said. "Focus on the stone. picture it moving away from you, and then command it to do so with a gesture."

Zak was too afraid to focus. After all the years of wishing and hoping he had magic, for the first time in his life he found himself happy he didn't have any. He wanted to be home. All he needed to do was show Sorwin there was nothing remarkable about him.

Without thinking, Zak flicked his hand, pouring all his pent-up emotions from the last day into the motion, wishing the stone would leave and go far, far away so he didn't have to feel anything anymore. Immediately the stone flew like a rogue star, hurtling straight toward the woods. Loud cracking noises sounded as it shot through several trees and out of sight, showing no sign of stopping.

The crowd of children gasped behind him. Zak's eyes opened wide, shock stunning him. *Three Fires!* What happened? Panic began setting in. He looked at the mage, who was staring right back and looking very intrigued with this new development. Before he knew what he was doing, Zak put his jade necklace on and turned, running home faster than ever.

"Zak!" Kal called after him, but it was no use. Zak was stopping for nothing and no one. He was running straight home and crawling in bed, hoping to fall asleep and wake up, finding this all to be another nightmare.

As he watched the young boy run from the field, Sorwin knew he had found who he was looking for. He also knew the Consortium wouldn't be far behind.

CHAPTER 3
TAKEN

Zak was running again. The night, the woods, the unnerving feeling, everything appeared exactly the same as it had for the last several weeks. Yet something was different this time. He was more conscious of his actions, but could do little to control them.

Suddenly there was an explosion, or he thought there was. He knew he heard one, and the heat of fire pressed against him, but he couldn't see what exploded or where it happened. Then he was shaking. No, not shaking, but being shaken.

"Zak!" He heard the distant call. His mother? What was happening?

The next instant he was awake in his room. Smoke billowed up the ladder from the house below and out through a gaping hole above. Pieces of the roof were scattered on his floor, starting small fires wherever they landed.

His mother was at his side, shaking him into consciousness. "Zak!" She cried again. "Oh thank Cerevita you're awake."

"What happened?" he asked.

"There's no time. Quickly now, we must leave this place!"

Zak and Clairise climbed down what was left of the ladder, slipping on a few rungs that snapped under their weight. All around them the house was aflame. The fire crawled up the beams, licking the timber frame greedily. The scorched wood hissed loudly in defeat, creaking and breaking under the torture as it was devoured.

Zak and Clairise heard Ageric yelling outside and headed to the front door, toward his voice. They burst from the front door as another explosion rocked the home, throwing them to the ground. As Zak skidded to a stop in the dirt, he instinctively looked skyward and saw a large black, winged figure dart across the sky.

"Run," Clairise said breathlessly. She saw the figure too. "Run as fast as you can away from here!"

Zak stared wide-eyed at his mother, shock stilling his comprehension.

"Go!" she commanded more forcefully.

Zak snapped to his senses, scrambled to his feet and ran toward town for help. Not twenty paces down the road the dark figure swooped in front of him and landed heavily, emitting a cackling laugh that stunned Zak with fear.

"Well-met, *Nacusti*," its gravelly voice said, spreading its black wings wide. Zak saw the figure was a man, a winged man. This was a Magerus, but it wasn't Sorwin. Two Mageri in Densba? What were they after?

"Who are you?" Zak managed to ask, stumbling backward. Sweat beaded on his forehead and his hands trembled.

It was too dark to discern many details of the man's form. He had dark hair, was tall, and Zak thought he saw dozens of tiny scars on his face, glinting slightly lighter than the rest of the man's skin in the firelight.

"Answering fool questions isn't part of my task," the man said. "But taking you is!"

He lunged forward, arms extended. Zak froze in place, unable to move. He was within the man's grasp, about to be abducted.

A beam of orange light blasted into the man's side, sending him careening off to the right. Zak swung his head around to see Sorwin landing gracefully by his side.

"Are you well? Are you uninjured?" Sorwin asked with urgency. His large golden wings shone bright against the darkness.

"F-fine," Zak stuttered. "Who is he? What is going on? What are you both doing here?" His head whirled from fear and confusion.

Sorwin answered with exactly the opposite response Zak needed. "I'll explain later. Right now you need to run and hide. You will be safest out of sight."

Zak covered his face as he was buffeted from the wind and dirt kicked up by Sorwin taking flight, pursuing the mysterious winged man.

He grimaced in frustration. *That's two people now telling me to run*, he thought as he ran headlong into the woods under cover of darkness. Remembering the intense fear he felt mere moments ago kept his pace steady. He ran west toward the river. He wasn't sure why, but it was the only place he could think of.

A few hundred yards from his house Zak felt an odd familiarity with his situation. It was dark, he was running, he couldn't see because there was no moon tonight, and he felt a presence behind him.

The dark figure!

This was his dream incarnate, one of his worst nightmares come to life and he had no idea how. The revelation distracted Zak and he tripped on an exposed root. He could hear something crashing violently through the treetops as he rolled over to see the winged man descending upon him. Fear paralyzed him again as he stared into his doom.

"Move!" Kal yelled. He ran in from the right, grabbing Zak by the shirt and pulling him upright, barely slowing his run as he did. Zak heard the winged man smash hard into the ground, followed by another loud crash he assumed was Sorwin. He didn't turn to find out, but instead kept running toward the river with Kal.

"Good timing," Zak said. "How did you know—"

"You'd need saving?" Kal finished. "You can barely pass history without me, why would escaping a life-threatening situation be any different?" Kal smiled, half joking. "That, and it was impossible to miss the explosions coming from your house." Zak heard the trepidation in his friend's voice. "What was that thing?"

"A Magerus," Zak said.

"Like Sorwin?"

"Yes, Sorwin is the one fighting him. I don't know who the man is, but he's after me for some reason. Sorwin told me to run and hide, but I hate that idea. I feel like I should do something."

"We have no place in a battle between Mageri," Kal said. "We'd only be in the way, or get ourselves killed. Best we take Sorwin's advice and hide. If the man is distracted with finding you, Sorwin will win, or at least drive him off."

"Do we know we can trust Sorwin though?" Zak asked, panting as he continued running and talking.

"Not this again. Look, I understand if you had doubts before, but they should be erased now. You said yourself Sorwin is fighting that mage who is trying to kidnap you."

"What if Sorwin just wants him out of the way so he can kidnap me instead?"

Kal looked at Zak like he was a loon.

"You're right," Zak agreed reluctantly, though the matter was far from settled in his mind. They continued on their path toward the river, running swiftly. "You saw my parents?"

"They're alive, fighting the fire. The mage does seem to only be after you as he's leaving everyone and everything else alone. I think the fire was meant as a distraction."

Zak wasn't comforted by that thought, but he found solace in the knowledge that no one was harmed. Then another thought crossed his mind.

"Kal, wait," he said, stopping his friend. They came to a halt just past the tree line of the forest near the river.

"What are you doing? We have to keep moving, the Magerus could find us here," Kal said, grabbing Zak's arm and pulling.

"No," Zak answered, pulling his arm back and breaking

Kal's grip. He squinted, trying to look into his friend's eyes. It was too dark to make anything out clearly. "Kal, if this mage is after me I can't let you stay near me. I can't put you at risk."

"Who said anything about 'letting' me stay? I'm a better fighter, so you can't knock me out and leave me. I'm faster than you, so you can't outrun me. As long as I want to help you, I'd say your options are limited."

"Kal…"

"I'm staying. It's decided."

"When did you become as stubborn as me?" Zak asked, obviously defeated.

"Good question, one I don't have the answer to for once. Now come on, let's keep moving."

"Wait a moment," Zak said again.

"Oh now what?" Kal asked harshly, turning back to him.

"Quiet, listen, don't you hear that?"

A soft song played on the wind, accompanied by whispers that spoke to Zak in a language unknown to him. They were the same voices he heard the night before. Was this why he was drawn to the river?

"I don't hear anything," Kal said. He eyed Zak curiously.

For a moment, Kal's voice sounded loud and strangely foreign to Zak. He strained to hear the song and voices again, but they were lost.

"We should find some cover," Zak said.

"Finally, words of wisdom."

They turned to run when a series of loud crashing noises erupted from the forest. Suddenly the winged man emerged, flying low and heading straight for Zak.

Zak's stomach dropped as fear flooded his body again. He turned and ran, his feet felt heavy and clumsy. He stumbled but stayed upright and kept moving. A quick glance back proved he wasn't fast enough. Zak's eyes widened as he saw the winged man's fiendish smile, arms outstretched once more, reaching for his prize.

Kal came out of nowhere, shoving Zak aside and standing in his place. Zak tumbled to the ground, rolling roughly to the side. The switch happened so fast and the night was so dark Zak wasn't sure the winged man saw what happened.

He had snatched Kal instead of Zak.

"No!" Zak yelled, standing and running after the winged man as he carried Kal away.

They sped away at a frightful speed, one Zak couldn't keep up with. He dropped to his knees, cursing his useless, fear-ridden body for failing to move fast enough. Cold evening dew soaked through his breeches, clinging icily to his legs. He didn't care, he was too overwhelmed with guilt. Kal was taken and it was *his* fault.

Just then Sorwin came running out of the woods. Zak's hope rose as the mage came to his side, checking him for injuries again. Surely he could help.

"Are you well?" Sorwin asked.

"Yes, but the winged man has Kalbick. Look!"

Sorwin cast his eyes up and saw the large, dark figure hurtling away with the outline of Kal's frame struggling beneath his captor.

"Hurry, we have to do something!" Zak shouted.

A shadow crossed the mage's face. "There's nothing we

can do, Zak," Sorwin said solemnly.

Zak's tone became even more desperate. "What do you mean? Chase him! He's getting away!"

"It would do no good. He has a large lead, and I can sense the portal he has open. He would escape before I even came close."

"Open your own portal! Chase him!" Zak begged. Tears streaked down his cheeks as he grabbed the mage's shoulders and shook.

"I can't...it doesn't work that way, Zakolor." The mage held him, offering what little comfort he could.

Zak sobbed for another minute. *It's my fault*, he thought. *Kal is gone because of me.*

Another voice rang in his thoughts, *Knock it off! You don't have time for this!* He shook his head. He couldn't feel bad for himself, not now. If Sorwin wouldn't help, Zak needed to get information. Information to save Kal himself.

"Who was he?" Zak managed to ask. He sniffed and wiped his nose with a sleeve, trying to compose himself.

"That was Burvenin, one of Zandorn's generals."

Zak lurched forward, resting his hands on his knees. He thought he would be sick as he rubbed the tears from his eyes. The knowledge that his best friend was in such dangerous custody added to his already considerable guilt.

He knew who Burvenin was—everyone in the four kingdoms did. He was Zandorn's right-hand man, known as the Silverfire General not only for the color of his flames, but for the state of his enemy when he was through with them. Little more survived his fire than the silver of their swords and armor, and sometimes not even that was spared.

"He's a Magerus," Zak said.

"Yes, he left Tor'alan nearly a century ago, right after Zandorn. You see, Zandorn was charged with studying the forbidden art of necromancy," Sorwin explained. "One who masters necromancy can master death itself. He promised immortality to Burvenin in exchange for helping him build his own nation, the Consortium."

Zak turned to the mage. "He called me *Nacusti*. Why? Why was he after me? Where is he taking Kal? Why are you really here?" He barraged Sorwin with questions, desperate for answers.

Sorwin hesitated before speaking. "I know you are frustrated, and that you have many more questions. I promise I will answer them all in time. First, we need to get back and help your parents put out the fires."

An image of his parents fighting flames crept into his mind. He couldn't let anyone else remain at risk because of him. As he looked to the mage to nod his agreement, he had his own hesitation. This was only his second encounter with Sorwin after the scouting session. Was he sure he could trust him?

"You're right," he said as he stood, brushing soil from his clothes. He moved toward the woods, toward his parents.

"It would be quicker if we flew," Sorwin suggested.

Zak stopped at the sound of his voice but didn't turn to face him.

"I'll run," he said. He wasn't sure if the venom in his reply was from distrust of the mage, anger with him for not even trying to pursue Burvenin, or anger at himself for getting Kal captured. Whatever the reason, he started running.

He was moving fast. Trees whipped by him as he skipped over roots and ducked under branches, the occasional leaf brushing his cheek. The wood was silent; not in a dangerous way, but in a respectful one. It was as if the forest knew how he felt and left him to his misery in peace.

Zak continued on his path and heard the mage's strong wings beating overhead. It seemed Sorwin was determined to keep a close eye on him. The thought spurred Zak to greater speed, running harder and faster, ignoring the pinch in his sides. Maybe if he exhausted himself he'd be too tired to feel anything.

CHAPTER 4
THE CHOICE

Zak made it back to his house panting heavily from the run and saw his parents, Joryl, and several other townspeople throwing buckets of water on what was left of the house. The attic was gone, as was half of the first floor. All that remained was the forge and part of the kitchen.

The rhythmic beating of Sorwin's wings went unnoticed by the townspeople as the mage landed gracefully next to Zak. He stepped forward, wanting to help save his home, but Sorwin gently stopped him with an outstretched arm.

"Let me," he offered.

Zak looked at the mage, his friendly face pinched in concern. He didn't trust him, not yet. Judging by the state of his house, though, he was not in a position to deny help. Zak nodded his consent and stepped back.

Sorwin closed his eyes and began muttering under his breath in a language Zak had never heard. He stared in awe as a stream of water began spiraling out from the mage's hands. It went toward the flames, swimming and twisting around the house to douse the fires.

The townspeople stopped what they were doing and stepped back, letting the mage do what they could not. Their amazement was even greater than Zak's, pointing and cheering as the water reduced the flames to harmless embers. When its deed was done, the stream evaporated, as though it had never been.

Then Sorwin began a new chant. As he did, scattered pieces of the house strewn across the yard flew back to their original places while material that was destroyed regenerated. Before the last smoke clouds cleared the house looked even better than before the fire ravaged it.

Stunned expressions covered the villagers' faces. They quickly gathered around the mage and thanked him profusely, as if he had fixed their own homes or delivered a miracle. To the people of Densba, this *was* a miracle. Magic of this level was a rare sight for them.

Zak watched as Sorwin graciously accepted their thanks with a genuine smile, shaking hands and complimenting many for their efforts. He was equally as astounded, and had to make an effort to close his gaping jaw. He wanted to trust the mage—at least he thought he did—but he needed questions answered first.

As the excitement died down, Sorwin spoke. "You can all rest easy. The threat has left, and the danger along with him."

Kal's parents pushed through the crowd, the concern on their faces grew by the second. They spotted Zak next to the mage and ran towards him.

"Have you seen Kal? He went off with you in the woods. Where is he? Has he come back yet?"

Zak's throat caught. "I...he..." He stood dumbfounded, lost for words. How could he deliver the worst news imaginable to his best friend's parents?

The longer he fumbled for an explanation, the less he needed one. As they stared at him, tears welled in Bill and Marralee's eyes. He tried to answer their pleas, but Sorwin cut in and saved him for the second time that evening.

"You must be Kal's parents," Sorwin surmised. The mention of Kal's name shifted their attention to the mage. Sorwin reached out and grasped one hand each of the grief-stricken parents. "You already know your son isn't here, but he is alive. He has been taken. I will do everything in my power to get him back. I will also explain everything to you, but right now I must speak with the Keldins. Can you wait for me in your home?" His tone was comforting and his expression soft. As Bill and Marralee nodded and turned they were immediately swallowed by a supportive group of townsfolk and shepherded to their home.

"Joryl," Sorwin said, spotting the council leader. "If you would wait for me at the inn I would speak to you before the night is through."

"Of course, Sorwin," Joryl agreed. "We thank you for your service." He shooed the remaining villagers back to their homes as he made his way to the inn.

Sorwin, Ageric, Clairise, and Zak stood in the yard of the restored home, only streaks of burned grass leaving any trace of the inferno. Zak's parents seemed conflicted; Clairise flattened her nightdress repeatedly while Ageric scratched at his beard. He realized they must be partially thankful to Sorwin for saving their home and their son, yet the mysterious man's warnings from years past to avoid anyone from the League seemed to give them pause. The tension between the four was palpable.

"Maybe we should go inside," Zak said, trying to bridge the gap between them all.

"Yes, of course," Clairise said. Her expression twisted for a moment in an effort to hide her hesitation. "How rude of us. Please, come in for tea. It is the least we can do after you saved our son and gave us our home back."

"Thank you," Sorwin said, accepting the offer and following them inside.

Even though the house appeared the same, it was entirely different. Maybe not different, Zak thought, but definitely newer. The floor no longer creaked by the hearth as his mother crossed the room to hang the kettle. The hinges on the windows and the finish on the woodwork shone with a newfound brilliance in the low lighting. As they sat at the table and waited for the water to boil, the old soup stain that used to mark Zak's place had vanished. A momentary smirk found his face as he was warmed by the magnificence of magic.

Clairise served the tea and took her seat by Ageric. Awkward introductions were made, and Zak knew this was going to be difficult.

"It is an honor to meet you both," Sorwin said to Clairise and Ageric. "I am Sorwin. The League Council sent me here under the guise of scout, but my true objective was to find your son."

"Why?" Ageric asked bluntly.

"He is the last *Nacusti*."

Silence extended the following moments to an unnatural length. *Nacusti*? That's what Burvenin called him. Why was the name familiar? Where had he heard it before?

"That's impossible!" Clairise argued. "The Belcour bloodline was extinguished—"

"Nearly eighteen years ago," Sorwin said. "How old are you, Zakolor?"

"My seventeenth was a few months back."

"Does he know?" Sorwin asked with a pointed look at Clairise and Ageric.

Ageric was stone-faced. The tension in his jaw and forehead made him appear tougher than the anvil in his shop. Clairise was turning redder by the second.

"I know," Zak said, answering for his parents before they imploded. "I know they're not my natural parents."

"Then you believe me when I say you're the last *Nacusti*?" Sorwin asked.

The meaning of the word came back to Zak and his eyes widened as he understood the weight of Sorwin's words. "You mean I'm...Guardian-born?"

"That is the direct translation, yes. Your mother was Kamira Belcour, descendant of Adrastus Belcour, receiver of the Blood Gift and champion of the Guardian War."

"But I have no magic, I can't be a Belcour. There must be some mistake." Shock and confusion gripped him tight.

"Ah, but you do have magic. We saw as much earlier during scouting. Did you forget about your demonstration with the stone already?"

"You went to the scouting session?" Clairise asked.

Zak gulped. "I had to, I thought Sorwin could tell me once and for all if I had any potential, or if maybe he could get information about my parents."

Clairise crossed her arms and huffed, leaning back in her chair. Zak knew she was angry with his disobedience, but he couldn't think of that now.

He turned his attention back to Sorwin, not about to let the mage stop talking now that he was finally getting answers. "Why did I have magic earlier today but never before?"

"Your necklace is spelled to contain your gifts."

"Why?"

"I think it best I start from the beginning," Sorwin said, taking a deep breath. "You were born in Florinshire, a small town on the northwestern plains. At that time, the Consortium was little more than a collection of renegade mages. The League pursued them and small conflicts occurred now and then, but no serious efforts were mounted to disband the group. Men have short memories, and this dispute had gone on longer than most had been alive.

"Shortly after your birth, Florinshire was attacked and the whole town destroyed. We believe the Consortium need-ed Belcour blood and would stop at nothing to get it. None of your kin survived, but you were rescued by Archmagus Tansil Windover. The attack on Florinshire reignited the war with the Consortium. Tansil knew as long as you were alive the Consortium would continue chasing you, and the League would covet your power for their own. He brought you to the port city of Bernadooth on this island in hopes of hiding you away."

"Tansil is the one who gave me away?" Zak barely processed the fount of new information.

"Yes."

"Why did he come back?" Ageric asked. His face was still taut.

Sorwin gave him a confused look.

"The necklace, why is it important?" Ageric rephrased.

"Ah yes, the jade," Sorwin said. "A few weeks after giving Zakolor to you, Tansil detected massive amounts of magical energy coming from the southern isles, near where you said you lived. He came here and discovered it was the child emitting the energy. Tansil's best guess was that Zak's magic was trying to protect him. He gave Zak the necklace to cloak him from detection and bind his gifts."

Zak looked down and found himself clutching the jade. Again the stone had slipped his mind, and again he thought it very strange. The confused look on Zak's face gave away his thoughts.

"It was also enchanted to be forgotten unless you focused on it. Tansil didn't want you to take it off for any reason and risk you being found by the Consortium," Sorwin explained.

"Yet they still found me," Zak said quietly, remembering Kal's sacrifice to save him.

"Your dreams overcame the enchantment, at least temporarily. It was made to contain your talents, but the dreams became focused strikes against the enchantment because your power tried defending you in your unconscious state.

"I'd love to enlighten you further," Sorwin continued, "but I'm afraid it's not safe. Any number of magical ears could be listening right now. Before our conversation ends, though, I need to ask you one thing. The Consortium knows where you are, and when they realize their mistake in taking Kal, you won't be safe here anymore. As I see it, you have two choices. You can come with me and hone your magic, or set out on your own. The choice is yours to make, but I would recommend against remaining here."

"You want me to come to the capital of the League and train with you?" Zak asked for clarification. If he wasn't in such mortal danger the stark difference between his life yesterday and his life today would be comical.

"Yes. Will you come to Tor'alan as my apprentice?"

"You expect us to leave our home, after everything that happened tonight?" Clairise asked, exasperated.

"I know it is an unfair request, but it truly is in your best interest," Sorwin said. "The Consortium will soon realize their kidnap attempt failed and return for their intended target."

"What of the townspeople? Are we to abandon them? Escape while they are caught in the middle of a conflict they have nothing to do with?" Ageric asked. His tone frightened Zak.

"The League will send reinforcements, I assure you. We will need to capture as many Consortium members as possible for questioning when they return here. Densba will not be left defenseless."

Ageric grunted, sounding unsatisfied. Zak could tell by

the rings under his father's eyes he was too tired to argue. As he looked at his parents' fearful faces he wondered how scarcely a day ago he could be so selfish as to wish for a grand adventure.

Zak thought hard for several moments. As Sorwin said, staying was not an option. He would simply put more people in danger. Running off on his own didn't seem viable, either. If Burvenin came back he definitely didn't stand a chance. Then there was Kal, kidnapped by the Consortium. Zak couldn't let that stand, couldn't sit idly by. He already promised himself he would get his friend back. He doubted he could do that without developing his magic. The choice was clear.

"I'll go with you," Zak said.

Clairise sighed heavily. "Come on then, Ageric. Let's start packing." His parents started rising from their chairs.

"No," Zak said.

"No?" Clairise parroted. "It's a long road to Tor'alan. We'll be needing supplies, dear."

"You're not coming," Zak said. He looked up from the spotless table and directly into his mother's eyes.

She stood unmoving. "What are you playing at?"

Zak kept a firm composure more for his sake than hers. Now was not the time to waver.

"You heard what Sorwin said, the Consortium is going to keep coming after me. I can't risk you coming with me and being in danger."

"We're your parents. We worry about your safety, not the other way 'round!" Clairise argued.

"This is bigger than parents and children. This is war, and I'm a target. Besides, you need to stay here and help Joryl. The Consortium will return, even after I leave, and someone will need to defend this new house Sorwin made for you."

Zak fought tears but Clairise could not. A few escaped her eyes and streaked down her face as Zak crossed to her and grabbed her hands.

"Knowing you are safe will keep me strong."

"How do *we* stay strong, then?" she asked.

"Apparently I am heir to a thousand year legacy. That must count for something," he said, breaking into a smile and wiping a tear from his mother's cheek.

Ageric stepped closer to Clairise, put one arm around her and grasped Zak's shoulder with the other. "We'll respect your decision, Zakolor. You're a fine young man."

Zak nodded his thanks. He and Ageric never needed to exchange many words. They understood one another. Clairise fled from the room in a flurry of sobs and Ageric pursued her.

Sorwin nodded understandingly. "I know that wasn't easy, and I'm sorry you've been given these circumstances."

Zak looked to the closed bedroom door behind which his mother continued to cry. "It was necessary. They're good parents, good people. I can't drag them into this more than they already have been." He faced the mage. "When are we leaving?"

"At first light. You should pack what you need and rest as much as you can."

"What do I need?" Zak had never traveled *anywhere* before.

Sorwin smiled. "Not much. The less the better. Extra clothes, mainly. I'll bring all of the practical supplies we'll need."

"What of Kal's parents? I have to tell them what happened," Zak said solemnly.

"I think you have endured enough for one day. I will speak to his family before retrieving my things from the inn." He hesitated for a moment before continuing. "You have to try not to blame yourself, Zak. You didn't ask him to save you."

"I know," he said unconvincingly.

"Salvage what you can of the night. I'll be back in a few hours." Sorwin slipped out of the house with near silence.

Zak slowly climbed the restored ladder to his room and collapsed on his bed. He stared at the ceiling where not even an hour before there was a gaping hole with smoke billowing out.

With answers to his questions came responsibilities, followed by more questions. He was the key to ending a hundred year war. He had a destiny. He was the *Nacusti*.

CHAPTER 5

OCEAN'S EMBRACE

Zak woke to the sound of banging pots and his mother's loud voice. He dressed and descended the ladder to find the source of her apparent anger.

"You'll need these to cook with on the road!" she yelled, throwing her cookware into a trunk that lay open on the floor. A few feet behind her stood Sorwin, a troubled yet understanding look on his face.

"Clairise, I assure you, I have enough pots to cook for us already," he said.

"But they're not my pots!" she said as she burst into a stream of sobs.

She was clearly having a difficult time adjusting to Zak's leaving. He calmly walked over to his mother and embraced her in a loving hug. She wrapped her arms around him and grasped tighter than he thought possible.

"I can't lose you," she whispered.

"You'll never lose me," he said, resting his chin on top

of her head. "We're just parting for a while, like we talked about."

"We can arrange to have you moved to Tor'alan once we're sure the road is safe," Sorwin offered.

Clairise wiped her eyes and put on a brave smile. The hug seemed to have a soothing effect and she calmed down enough to be embarrassed.

"I am sorry, Sorwin, I've lost my head a bit," she apologized.

"Of course you have, it is to be expected," he said comfortingly. "Honestly, I think you're doing rather well given the gravity of the situation."

Clairise stood a little straighter. "It's what we do here in Densba. We move forward no matter the situation, gravity or no. I'll go speak with Ageric about moving to Tor'alan." She brushed her hand softly across Zak's cheek before leaving the room.

Zak's brow furrowed and he felt a twinge in his chest as his eyes followed her out of the room. He knew leaving his parents was going to be difficult, but he didn't think it would hurt this much.

Sorwin let out a large sigh. "Are you all packed?" His tone was almost too upbeat for Zak's current mood.

"Yeah, I did it last night. I didn't get much sleep."

"Much to be expected, I'm afraid. Once we're traveling all day I'm sure sleep will come easier."

"Yeah, I guess," he said halfheartedly.

Did he even want to sleep anymore? Apparently the energy released during his dreams lured Burvenin right to his house. Knowing his dreams were so dangerous he thought it would be better if he never slept again. Thinking about his dream and last night's events sparked a thought.

"Is it possible for someone to have a dream and then live it? Or to have dreams come to life?" he asked, turning to face Sorwin.

"Well, sure. There are all sorts of spells to take things from your subconscious and make them physical realities. You could also go on a dream walk to fully understand a dream, or you could do it for entertainment if you had a really good dream and wished to revisit it. I believe there is also a spell for—"

"No," Zak said, harsher than he intended. "I mean, say you have a dream one night and then the next day your dream actually happens, without any magic involved."

"Ah. Yes, that is entirely different. Is that what happened to you?" he asked. Zak noticed Sorwin's eyes flashed with a brightness, perhaps curiosity.

"I think so. I've been having the same dream for the past few weeks now, it was the attack in the forest."

"How intriguing!" Sorwin exclaimed. "What you have been experiencing is Sight magic. It is a rare gift that allows a person a glimpse of the past, present, or future. The fact that you could use Sight magic while sleeping and wearing the jade is impressive."

Zak sensed the mage's excitement. Sorwin ran a hand through his hair in what Zak took to be an attempt to calm himself down. *He must really love magic,* Zak thought.

"Right," Zak said. He frowned, conflicted. He was excited at the notion of possessing such an incredible gift, but how could he keep it under control if it happened while he was sleeping?

Sorwin seemed to pick up on his thoughts.

"We'll start your training on the road to help you learn control," Sorwin said. "It may be best to keep the jade on when we're not training, just for now. I'll reinforce the enchantment to account for your dreams. We wouldn't want to risk any outbursts before we reach Tor'alan."

Zak nodded his agreement. "I don't want to put anyone else in danger."

He looked up and saw Sorwin nodding as well, his eyes staring at the floor, but they were seeing something else. At that moment, Zak had an odd feeling that Sorwin was the only person who understood his burden.

Another hour passed before Zak and Sorwin were on the road, trotting at a healthy pace on the backs of fresh horses. The goodbyes with his parents were painful, and Zak worked to push the fresh memories from his mind. Instead, he focused on the present and his impending future.

The road they traveled was well-worn but sturdy, giving them little trouble. Tall pines lined up like soldiers to the right as the left opened into a serene valley, huge boulders dotting the landscape. It was a clear day, and the crisp morning air coupled with the scenery slightly improved Zak's mood. A hawk circled overhead and dove to the earth, snatching some unaware prey. After a few hours of riding they stopped at a small stream for a short break.

When Zak dismounted his legs wobbled beneath him.

He had ridden before and was considered somewhat skilled in the saddle, but he wasn't accustomed to longer treks and didn't have the rider's endurance. As he stretched his muscles and walked to loosen up, Sorwin approached him.

"Why don't you take the necklace off for a minute, Zak?"

He paused momentarily, conscious of the risks, but removed the jade and put it in his pocket. He promised himself he would find Kal. He needed to learn control of his gifts if he hoped to do so.

"What do you know of magic, of how it works?" Sorwin asked.

"I know magic is in everything—people, animals, plants, the earth." He recited one of his school lessons from memory.

"Very good, what else?"

Zak thought harder. The knowledge, the facts, this was Kal's strength. Zak had always learned best by doing.

"I know all mages can use fire," he said. Zak wasn't sure how he knew that, the thought came to him as if remembering something he forgot.

Sorwin's normally jovial eyes narrowed, flickering with suspicion for a moment. His face quickly returned to normal as he spoke again.

"Yes, that's correct. Magic is, fundamentally, about intention. Coincidentally, fire is where we'll begin your studies. Before you can work a spell you'll need to connect with your magic. Do you know what that means?"

Zak shook his head. Whatever intuition he had a moment ago was gone.

"Magic is essentially a person's core. It's different from

their soul, but we won't get into the details now. I want you to close your eyes and focus. Focus on reaching your magic and connecting with it."

Zak did as requested, closing his eyes. His breathing was steady and his thoughts were noisy. They kept drifting to Kal, his responsibility to his friend and his family, his fears and excitement about his new powers.

After several minutes Zak acknowledged these thoughts and let them pass. He realized he couldn't quiet his mind, but he didn't have to engage the thoughts, either. He split his mind in two: one passive to collect his thoughts, and one intent on finding his magic. He doubled his focus, searching for the energy. He could feel it was there, bobbing just out of reach like he was chasing it through shallow water. It was ahead of him, diving deeper just before he came upon it.

His brow furrowed and a bead of sweat streaked his right temple. As he was about to give up, he found it.

Zak's magic felt warm. It reminded him of the first time he saw the ocean. The expanse of water stretched for miles and miles. His magic felt the same way, like it was endless. He knew enough about magic to know it wasn't endless, that all mages had a finite amount of energy.

"I have it," he said quietly, afraid he might break the connection with a sudden movement or speaking too loud.

"Good," Sorwin said. "Now, raise your arm above your head, open your eyes, and pull on your magic, just a little. Guide the energy to your hand and say, '*tegoperignis*'. It's a spell that will create a protective shield."

Zak followed Sorwin's instructions. He pulled on his

magic, but it was resistant to move at first, like a lazy cat waking from a nap. He managed to work a thin thread from the mass of energy and pulled gently. Once the small piece started to move, the rest wanted to follow. Much more of his magic than he intended flooded up to his hand.

Zak panicked and yelled, "*Tegoperignis!*"

He opened his eyes as green fire sprouted from his hand and whirled around Zak, shrouding him in a protective orb. The fire whipped around him, lashing out at random as if it were attacking invisible enemies. Zak looked at Sorwin, panic quickening his breath. "Focus your mind, Zakolor. Focus on creating a smooth surface. Rein in the extra magic and fire." Sorwin had to yell his instructions as the fiery torrent whipped loudly through the air.

Zak closed his eyes again and focused on stemming the flow of magic. He imagined a door to his energy. He closed the door nearly all the way, leaving it open just a crack. The tiny sliver of essence managed to sneak through while he held back the rest that wanted to escape.

When the source felt stable, he opened his eyes again and noticed the fire was much calmer.

"See if you can smooth the surface a bit," Sorwin said. "A tighter shield is more impervious to attacks."

Zak diverted a small part of his attention from controlling the flow of his magic to further smoothing the surface of his shield.

After a few more moments of sustaining the spell, Zak's knees buckled. He dropped his hand to catch himself and the flames expired simultaneously. He sat on the ground in the middle of a scorched circle, breathing hard in a shirt darkened by sweat. His head ached with the mental and magical efforts of casting his first spell.

"Very well done, Zakolor." Sorwin stepped over the fire-marked earth and handed Zak a waterskin. Zak took several large swigs to quench his thirst.

"Is magic always this exhausting?" Zak asked.

Sorwin smiled. "It depends on the spell, but no—you'll develop stamina over time."

"Good," Zak nodded. He stood as his expression hardened with determination. "Let's try again."

Sorwin's head tilted slightly, possibly with surprise or skepticism. "Are you sure?" he asked. "We still have a lot of road to travel today, and—"

"I'm sure," Zak said, trying to keep his voice steady. "I need to practice control, you said it yourself." Zak realized he wasn't breathing as he waited for Sorwin to react. He could only guess at the thoughts whizzing through the mage's mind.

Sorwin gave him a single nod. "Once more, then we move on," he agreed.

Zak nodded in return and closed his eyes, reaching for his magic once again.

Karazul watched from the shadows of a high peak, his sight magically enhanced, as the teacher and student practiced their craft. He had a small frame and could be considered short for the average man, but his build allowed quick movements, serving him well as an assassin.

Twin short swords clung to his back, both hilts wrapped in smooth leather. It was obvious the swords and their owner had seen many battles and taken many lives.

The Consortium employed Karazul to follow a boy named Zakolor. This was strictly an information gathering task, one he thought was beneath him until seeing the boy's magus. The sight of a Magerus piqued the deadly assassin's interest, and suddenly he was not so discontented with accepting this task.

This boy must truly be valuable, he mused. Maybe it was time to find out why.

He pulled a small black figurine from his pack. It was a two-headed wolf with the body of a man. Karazul ran his fingers over the carved surface, the obsidian smooth despite the etchings. The stone was so dark it seemed to absorb any light that touched it.

Karazul muttered a few words and dark smoke poured from the figurine, swirling in a small cyclone. When it cleared, two large wolves nearly the size of horses stood in front of him. Low, rumbling growls sounded from the beasts as their eyes quickly scanned their surroundings.

"Enough. I have a job for you," Karazul said with a smirk.

After a day of riding Zak was happy when Sorwin had them stop to make camp for the night. They settled in a small alcove a few dozen yards off the main road. Within an hour the horses were fed, bedrolls were set, and salted meat and potatoes simmered and crackled over a small fire.

"How are you feeling?" Sorwin asked. Wielding a large cooking fork, he pushed the contents of the pan around every few minutes.

"I'm fine," Zak lied. His muscles rebelled against him when collecting firewood earlier, forcing him to drop his bounty several times. He wasn't sure if Sorwin noticed. "Is there something I can practice while we wait for dinner?"

Sorwin didn't respond for a few moments. He added spices to the pan, causing a hiss and a new delicious smell to emit from the concoction.

"There is one thing you could try if you're sure you have the energy."

"I do," Zak said. "I need to keep progressing, for Kal."

"Just don't forget to continue *learning* while progressing." A sharp look accompanied Sorwin's warning. "You'll do Kal no good if you push past your limits before you're ready."

Zak looked down and nodded, his face warmed with embarrassment. Apparently Sorwin did notice his battle with the firewood earlier.

Sorwin sighed. "However, your motivation suits our cause. Unfortunately you will have to learn as much as possible as fast as possible. You are a target, *Nacusti*, and you will need to defend yourself too soon for my liking."

Zak flinched. "Could you...is it possible to not call me *Nacusti*?" he asked.

Sorwin's eyebrows raised slightly. "Of course," he quickly

agreed. "May I ask why?"

"Burvenin called me that right before he took Kal," Zak said. "I know it's what I am, but I'm not sure I like the name."

Sorwin nodded and took another breath before continuing. "As for what you can do now, every mage must learn how to meditate. This is how we control our power, learn to use it, and make it grow."

Zak noticed a more jovial Sorwin reappearing as he began sharing knowledge with Zak.

"Let's have you walk through the same steps as earlier when you were casting your spell. Quiet your thoughts, find your magic, but instead of pulling and using your magic, try to connect with it, to shape it."

"How? What do you mean 'shape it'?" Zak asked.

"You'll see—just try." A quick smirk crossed Sorwin's face.

Zak closed his eyes. He went through the steps Sorwin had instructed him on earlier that day. Steady, deep inhales and exhales, clearing his mind and focusing solely on his breath as it entered and left his lungs.

Next, he thought about the magic inside of him, *his* magic, and searched for it as he had before. He found the vast ocean of energy quicker this time, which made him happy to think he had already made progress.

Following Sorwin's instructions, he didn't pull on his essence this time. Instead, he reached out and touched it. Ripples waved through his magic in response. He felt the connection Sorwin mentioned—like all his magic was suddenly accessible.

What did Sorwin mean by 'shape it,' though?

How do you shape an ocean? he wondered. He explored the connection with his magic for several more minutes, feeling ripples wax and wane. He had an idea.

To rein in the mass, he pictured his magic as a small ball of energy. He cupped his hands and started coaxing the ocean-like energy into them. It went slowly at first, but as he grew more comfortable with the thought and the image was more solid in his mind, the magic flooded faster and faster into his hands until it was a small, green orb.

Manipulating the energy in this tiny shape was hard at first, it seemed to have a mind of its own. It jutted out randomly and tried to escape his hands, so Zak had to focus his thoughts and bend it to his will. Sometimes it ran away from him, almost taunting him to chase it. When he would catch it, he played with its shape, expanding and contracting it, moving it around.

From the recesses of his mind came a painful reminder of his physical exhaustion. His body ached in places he didn't know existed. While distracted, the little green orb began rapidly expanding, pouring out of his hands to resume the original ocean-like form. The sudden force of his magic expanding shocked him out of his meditative state.

When he opened his eyes, he was covered in sweat for the second time that day. He wasn't sure how long he had meditated, but Sorwin held a half-eaten plate of meat and potatoes.

"How did it go?" Sorwin asked.

"I'm not really sure," Zak said. "I'm tired and I feel like I hardly did anything."

Sorwin smiled. "I'm sure you did well. I could sense your magic humming. Meditating is exhausting until you learn how to connect fully with your magic. Eventually, it will be very rejuvenating."

He took another bite of potato. The food had apparently restored even more of Sorwin's personality as he continued. "Did you know that some mages don't actually sleep, they just meditate? Isn't that amazing? You see, what they do is…"

Zak smiled as his eccentric but knowledgeable magus continued on one of his tangents, which Zak was learning was a fairly frequent occurrence.

He was glad Sorwin found and rescued him and his family from Burvenin's clutches, but there were still so many unanswered questions that Sorwin said he would have to ask Archmagus Tansil once they reached the capital. Who was he really? What was his heritage? Who was his birth family? He thought the curiosity would drive him mad.

Shaking the thoughts from his head, he stood and stretched, walking to the fire to fill a plate for himself. He ate quickly, satisfying the hunger pains in his stomach, while Sorwin continued his meditation lesson with excited oration. Zak eventually interrupted long enough to say goodnight, crawled into his bedroll, and fell into a deep sleep, his first in many weeks.

Chapter 6

INNER FIRE

Zak was roused by the sound of Sorwin making break-fast: pots and pans clattered, different foods sizzled and boiled, and logs hissed as they fed the fire. After the fortifying meal, Zak and Sorwin packed the camp and set off at a healthy pace. There were no towns on their path to Bernadooth, so they met few—if any—travelers along the way.

While riding, Sorwin continued explaining magic and its principles and also teaching Zak minor spells, charms, and magical vocabulary. On the rare occasion they stopped for a break, Zak practiced his shield spell and the other magics Sorwin introduced.

"That brings us to the third law of inter-planar move-ment: Displacement," Sorwin said. He rode with his eyes ahead, apparently reciting from memory. "This law states that nothing can move between planes without an equal entity left behind to fill the void created by the displacement."

"What do you mean an 'equal entity'?" Zak asked.

"Well, it could mean a number of things, really. Most common is energy, but—" Sorwin abruptly stopped his steed, his head and eyes darting back and forth across the nearby treeline.

"What is it? What's wrong?" Zak stopped just behind the mage. He looked to the same spot but couldn't see anything.

"I'm not sure," Sorwin replied.

"Could be a deer?" Zak offered, though he didn't believe in his own optimism given the circumstances.

A flutter of movement caught his attention. As he looked to the spot, another movement a few yards closer distracted him.

"I don't think it's a deer," Sorwin said. His voice was low and quiet. "When I say, I want you to—"

Before he could finish, two large wolf-like creatures sprang from the trees and launched themselves toward Sorwin. His horse reared and caught the bulk of the attack, but threw him to the ground.

He quickly got to his feet, muttering a spell. One beast shook its head, recovering from the collision with the horse. The other circled its prey, turning from the mage to Zak.

Zak's eyes widened. The beast ran toward him, halving the distance in seconds. He yanked the jade from his neck, trying to remember one of the spells Sorwin taught him.

His mind was blank from panic. He caught a glance of Sorwin striking down the other wolf with a well-placed lightning bolt, which tore a hole through the beast's chest. It slumped heavily to the ground, lifeless. He looked back to the other wolf just as it leapt toward him.

He tried to recall a spell, but fear muddled his mind. He threw his hands up in front of his face in a meager defense. At least, he *thought* it was meager.

Just as the beast's giant maw was about to close on him, emerald-colored flames erupted from Zak's hands and smacked the wolf, causing it to hurtle harmlessly to the ground. Zak realized he was unscathed, and confusion and astonishment washed over him. Bewildered, he looked from his hands to the scorched animal that lay on the ground a few yards away, and then to his magus.

Sorwin ran over to the scalded but still living wolf, drew his sword, and swiftly decapitated the beast. Both bodies melted into black smoke that slithered swiftly back through the woods. The mage turned to a still surprised and stunned Zak.

"Are you all right?" he asked, running to Zak and checking him for injuries. This was becoming a far too regular occurrence in the short time they knew one another.

"I, I'm fine," Zak said, "but what were those things? And how did I..." he started to ask, trailing off as he stared at the place on the ground where the burned body used to be.

"It seems you've discovered another method of spellcasting, one I thought you weren't quite ready for. Apparently you are, though.

"You've already learned a few spells using power words, but it is also possible to incarnate magic with sheer willpower. It's a riskier form because it relies exclusively on the caster's thoughts, but it often produces more powerful effects. Tell me, what were you thinking of just now, right before you were attacked?"

Zak hesitated for a moment, trying to recall what had

passed through his mind. Most of it was a blur, but he did remember his intentions.

"I was thinking of yesterday, when I was practicing the flame shield spell. I wanted to cast it again but I couldn't get the word out in time."

"That would explain the flames," Sorwin confirmed.

Zak thought for another minute about the attack. "What were those things?"

"Those were Shadoweres, dangerous beasts, they are. The problem is the only way to kill them permanently is to destroy the statue from which they are summoned." The mage's brow furrowed. Zak knew him well enough now to recognize his worried face.

"What's bothering you? I mean, besides the fact we were almost killed, again," Zak asked.

"Well that's just it, isn't it?" Sorwin said. "We know the Consortium doesn't want you dead. They went to great lengths to try and kidnap you. This seems like a reckless action inconsistent with their goals."

"Do you think someone else is after us?"

"No, it doesn't seem likely. I doubt anyone else could have followed us. I think it means we have far more dangerous pursuers than I anticipated."

Sorwin's words landed heavily upon Zak. Even though he was almost kidnapped before, he felt safe since traveling with Sorwin. He was one of the most powerful mages in Valecium, after all. Now, someone was following them, watching them, and didn't seem to care if Zak lived or died. Only with a stroke of luck did he survive this attack.

His stomach twisted in knots with the realization he wasn't safe, and never was, not even with Sorwin.

"Should we keep moving? Or should we try and find this pursuer?" His voice quivered, unable to keep the fear out of it.

"I could track the beasts' path back to their statue, which may lead us to them, but it would take precious time. Whoever summoned them will most likely be moving fast, elongating the tracking process. We haven't the time to waste, and being that we're only one more day from Bernadooth I suggest we hurry and pray for no further attacks. I will increase our defenses which will hopefully ward off our pursuer."

Nodding his agreement, Zak nudged his horse down the path while Sorwin put up more wards. The pair rode in silence, keeping wary eyes on the trees and paying heed to every shadow.

Karazul leaned casually against a tree as the defeated shadoweres returned to him, the obsidian smoke flowing into the small statue in his hand. Behind Karazul stood a large rock face. It began glowing a light blue and moving rhythmically, as if part of the rock was actually water. A moment later, Burvenin stepped out from the blue, shimmering rock face.

"What have you done?!" Burvenin barked at Karazul.

"I thought I sensed a portal here, should have known it would be you," Karazul said.

"Your assignment is to *watch* and *gather information*, not assassinate the boy."

"My assignment is to evaluate his strength," Karazul retorted. He still leaned against the tree, not facing Burvenin, enjoying his subtle act of disrespect.

"The beasts could have easily killed him."

"It was a risk, I'll admit." Karazul finally turned. "But if this boy is as important as you and your master claim he is, I figured he would survive. And we weren't disappointed, were we? I'm actually a little impressed. A few days with the Hawk mage and the kid is conjuring fire on the spot. How exciting," he added drily.

Burvenin snarled and took a step toward Karazul. He was a full head taller and towered over the small assassin. "The Consortium will not tolerate—"

"The Consortium *must* tolerate, actually. That's the deal I have with your master. My assignment, my methods." Karazul looked up directly into Burvenin's eyes, silently daring the mage to challenge him.

"We will be rid of you soon, Void, and then I can deal with you using *my* methods," Burvenin said.

"I look forward to you trying," Karazul said. "I—" he paused, whipping around to look behind him. He felt a sudden and strong magical presence, but nothing was there.

"What is it, Void? Lose your wit?" Burvenin asked.

Karazul squinted, but he couldn't see anything. The feeling passed as quickly as it came over him. Whatever was there was gone now.

"It's nothing," he said. "Here." He took out a small piece of parchment and made some etchings with a piece of charcoal. "Take this to your master, he will know what it means."

Burvenin grunted but obeyed, snatching the parchment from Karazul. He turned and walked through the portal, and the rock face returned to normal after he was gone.

Karazul looked back to the spot where he felt the presence, frowning. "Curious. Seems I'm not the only one doing the following."

CHAPTER 7

BERNAD⊙⊙TH

Zak sighed heavily with relief. After another night of camping in the countryside and another day of hard traveling behind them, Zak and Sorwin rode into the bustling streets of Bernadooth, weary and exhausted. It was Zak's first time in a city, and though he felt nervous amongst the throng of bodies and unfamiliar sounds and smells the city had, he also felt safer. Maybe he felt less likely to be attacked here than in the countryside.

The city sat on the northern tip of the island, connected to the main island by a narrow strip of land. Zak thought it was a well-organized city with many rows of buildings; most were made of brick or stone and reached two or three stories. They seemed massive compared to the small wooden houses in Densba.

The cobblestone streets were well-used but sturdy. Zak and Sorwin pushed their way through the busy evening crowd to get to the Pig's Snout Inn, a three story wooden and plaster building. Just outside, Sorwin sold the horses to a merchant for seventeen silver League Marks each.

"We won't need them anymore, we'll be taking a ship to the mainland," Sorwin explained. He put the money from the sale in a small leather purse and handed it to Zak, who returned the gesture with an astonished look.

"The horses were from your village, right? Seems fair you should keep it." He smiled as he turned and entered the inn.

Zak nodded absently, never having held more than a few coppers before. He followed Sorwin inside the Pig's Snout, a few silver Marks richer.

The scent of ale and roasted meats and vegetables was the first thing Zak noticed. It was also warmer inside with a roaring fire in a stone fireplace in the center of the room. Half a dozen wooden tables with accompanying chairs crowded the inn's floor.

As Zak walked through the room, he could see the wear in the building and the furniture: the floors were scuffed, chips were missing from tables, chairs creaked as patrons shifted their weight. However, he could also tell the proprietor—or someone who worked here—really cared for the place. Tables were mended and the floor was buffed to shine where possible. It wasn't much, but it was important to someone.

The obvious care and devotion to the inn reminded Zak of Clairise. She showed the same pride in her own humble home, and a pang in his chest told Zak how much he missed his parents.

Sorwin finished speaking with the innkeeper and turned, handing him a key.

"I've arranged separate rooms for us. I thought you could use a night to yourself after several on the road with me."

Zak wasn't sure if this was the mage's attempt at a joke or not, but Sorwin was smiling (as always), so he returned the smile with his thanks. He was grateful to have a night alone to recover from the whirlwind of experiences from the last few days.

He followed Sorwin upstairs and they each entered small adjacent rooms. Zak closed the door behind him and evaluated his lodging.

Similar to downstairs, the walls were dark brown wood with sparse patches of plaster that showed their age. The room was longer than it was wide, with a small bed on the left side and a single window at the opposite end of the room. Zak dropped his things on the floor and briefly looked out the window.

He wished he had more energy. He would normally have jumped at the chance to explore the city, taste exotic foods, see a play—which he heard about repeatedly over the years from the time Kal had seen one.

Zak sighed again.

"I'm coming for you, Kal," he quietly promised to himself.

CHAPTER 8
WILLPOWER LOST

Kalbick's stomach growled. It had been nearly a day since the last feeding time. The guards should be coming through with more scraps any minute.

How long had he been here...two weeks? Three? A month? It was hard to tell. Passage of time in a dungeon was painful at best. It was best to pay it no mind.

He didn't remember much about how he arrived. He knew he was abducted, he remembered being at the river with Zak. After that, nothing but fractured images and guesswork filled in his foggy memories.

From bits and pieces of conversations he recalled he wasn't the intended target, Zak was. Why did they want his friend? What was so special about him? It was odd that he suddenly had magic at this year's scouting. Was that it? Whatever it was, it must have been for the same reason Sorwin went to their small town. He remembered hearing the words "rare" and "good for something," but they meant little without context.

His head still felt heavy and cloudy from the magic that

kept him sedated during his transport. There was only one positive to Kalbick's situation: he was the newest member of the cell he inhabited with four other boys, all roughly his age. They were all far more ragged and weary than Kalbick, which was to his advantage come feeding time.

The guards slid four bowls of food into the cell, leaving one prisoner with no food. They watched the five boys scuffle and attempt to fight for their meals, betting on who would be left with nothing.

When Kalbick first arrived, he tried to share the food amongst all the boys. The others wouldn't have it, instead choosing to punch him in the eye and take his share. After two days of attempted peace talks, Kalbick's stomach got the better of him and his resolve hardened. He needed to be physically aggressive and emotionally detached to survive. With Kal's physical and mental prowess, he didn't miss a meal again after that second day.

Today, the odds would change. Three new prisoners were brought in and thrown into the cell. They looked identical, and Kalbick guessed they were triplets.

Great, he thought, almost certain they would band together to get as much food as possible.

In less than ten minutes, the guards came back with seven bowls of food and slid them inside the cell. Kalbick and the other veteran prisoners sprang towards the bowls, claiming meals and devouring them as quickly as possible.

The triplets, being new, took a moment to figure out what was happening. Once they did, Kalbick's prediction came true. They headed for the weaker of the prisoners, trying to steal their bowls. Two of the three held a prisoner down, beating him a sufficient amount to ensure he stayed down while the third ate the food. They rotated through holding and beating so they all had turns to eat.

Once they worked through the rest of the prisoners they came towards Kalbick, who had eaten most of his bowl already. He glanced up and growled at the advancing trio, showing the feral attitude he had acquired in the weeks of confinement. Kalbick heard the guards laughing and placing further bets, which only fueled his anger.

Kalbick's growl slowed the triplets for a second, but they continued toward him, backing him into a corner as they tried to flank him. They made a few attempts to grab the bowl, but Kalbick held his defense, counter swinging and trying to keep them off balance. Even in his weakened state he was an excellent fighter and was more than a match for any one of these boys.

Kalbick knew, however, that he wouldn't be able to keep this up for long. They were freshly captured and there were three of them, and he would eventually tire. With every swing they stepped closer and closer.

He had to think quickly. Remembering what little training he had from Fenton, he thought back to the spells he was taught and how to work them. Finding the one he wanted, he reached for the diminished energy that was his magic and pulled forth as much as possible before muttering *"Fumus."*

As he did so, he blew air out of his mouth. It turned into a thick, dark blue fog that engulfed the entire cell. Under the cover of the smoke, Kalbick was able to deal at least one solid strike to each boy before retreating to finish his meal. The boys groaned on the ground, rolling in pain.

The guards opened the cell, shouting once they recovered from their surprise of seeing the magic. They cleared the smoke and dragged Kalbick out of the cell.

"Think yer pretty clever, eh? Wait til Zandorn is done with ye, then we'll see who's clever!" grunted one of the guards. Two of them dragged him by the elbows down the hall.

"Get off!" Kalbick yelled. He wriggled and fought their grips as much as possible but he was too weak to put up much resistance.

In all his time here, Kalbick had seen little beyond his cage. They were being kept in a cave of some sort. Everything was carved from stone and the entire place felt cool and damp. Their rapid footsteps echoed ahead of them down the many passageways that twisted into a labyrinth.

While he was being dragged, he could hear and see that there were dozens of other cells like his own, each occupied by several boys and girls that fought for their meals. Why? What was the purpose? He hadn't the energy or focus to figure it out now, and was more worried about where he was being taken, anyway. Prisoners had a way of disappearing and not returning around here.

As the guards rounded the corner they stopped abruptly. A slender girl with raven-black eyes and deep purple hair of almost the same hue stood in front of them. Her skin was white as quartz and she seemed to glow in the dimly-lit hallway. She was of average height but rare beauty.

The guards were shaking as she looked between them and him. He thought she couldn't have been more than a few years older than him. Why were the guards giving her so much respect, so much fear?

"Where are you taking this prisoner?" she asked, with a stern yet quizzical expression on her face.

"We're taking him to Lord Zandorn," answered the guard in front, more forcefully than necessary. He seemed to act more confident than he was.

Picking up on this, the girl smiled and asked "Oh, whatever for?"

The guard in front looked back to the two holding Kalbick for reassurance. "He used magic to attack some other prisoners. He'll need to be dealt with by Lord Zandorn."

"Interesting," the girl said flatly. She leaned to her left so she could see around the guard and better observe Kalbick.

He stared right back.

Apparently she was impressed, or at least intrigued, for she said, "Bring him to my chambers. I'll see that he makes it to my father."

Kalbick's eyes opened wide and his mouth dropped open slightly. He tried to gain his composure, but was very shocked to hear her use the term "father" in reference to Zandorn.

He didn't know much about Zandorn. He knew he committed some crime, something to do with necromancy, nearly a century ago and left Tor'alan to pursue his dark magic. He knew Zandorn was at war with Tor'alan and the various magic orders and kingdoms of Valecium. He didn't know he had a daughter.

"But, my lady, we're under strict orders to bring any prisoner who has used magic to see—"

"My father, yes, I know. He'll make it there, I promise," she said.

Kalbick thought her patience was thinning by the second as she said, "Gunther, please relieve these fine gentlemen of their cargo."

As she finished her command, a huge, ghostly figure lumbered out of the hallway directly to her left. Each of the guards backed up a step.

Gunther was close to seven feet tall, if not taller. His long, drawn face and stringy white hair indicated years of hardship. A quiet, almost sad grace accompanied his movements.

Kalbick had the feeling Gunther enjoyed working for the girl, though something felt amiss with his demeanor.

The guards released Kalbick as Gunther picked him up with one arm around his belly, holding Kalbick at his hip. From this new vantage point, Kalbick was at eye-level with the guards and could clearly see the trepidation on their faces.

"Thank you, that will be all," said the girl, politely dismissing the guards with a smile as if they had done her a great kindness.

"Yes, m-my lady," mumbled the guard in front before bowing and retreating quickly, glancing over his shoulder every few strides. The other two followed quickly behind.

"That really never gets old, does it, Gunther?" she asked, smiling up at the giant man.

"Hmph" was all Gunther said in return, and the girl looked down the hallway to the fleeing guards, apparently still pleased with herself.

"Well, let's move along, shall we, Gunther? And you, what's your name, boy?"

Caught unawares from finally being addressed personally, Kalbick cleared his throat.

"Uh, I'm Kalbick."

She smiled and said, "Well, it's a pleasure to meet you, Kalbick. I'm Renna, Zandorn's daughter, as I'm sure you heard. How would you like a square meal before going to meet him?"

"Yes, I'm ravenous!" he said, with more interest than he intended.

She smiled again and beckoned Gunther, the three of them moving through a maze of passageways until they arrived at a cave that opened into a space filled with light.

It was as if a giant hole had been carved out of the side of a mountain. The spacious room looked down on a small waterfall and a luscious forest with many fruit trees and bushes. Birds chirped and flitted through the air, and Kalbick even saw a few small animals scurrying along the forest floor below.

A large table nearly twenty paces in length was pushed right to the edge of the drop-off, overlooking the beautiful scenery. It was dressed with the finest feast Kalbick had ever seen, with roasted bird and glazed desserts and fruit so plump it looked about to burst with the slightest touch. He had to squint to see everything. It had been weeks since daylight last touched his skeletal body, and his eyes had almost forgotten how to adjust to the sun. Within a few minutes, his sight recovered and he was gorging himself on the generous spread.

Renna picked at a salad and watched Kalbick while Gunther stood behind her right shoulder.

After inhaling a few plates of food and two goblets of fresh pemberry juice, Kalbick slowed and began to think, curiosity restored by his sated stomach.

"Why did you take me from the guards?" he asked, wincing at how unappreciative he sounded.

Renna apparently knew what he meant, and answered without offense. "Honestly, you fascinate me. It's true that any prisoner who uses magic must be taken to my father, but I thought a small detour wouldn't hurt. Besides, it's been ages since anyone has shown as much promise as you."

"Promise for what?" he asked, still focusing on his food but becoming more intrigued by where the conversation was going.

"Why, promise for the future, of course. Tell me, do you know where you are right now? Or how you came to be here?" she asked.

He thought for a moment. "I was abducted and brought here by General Silverfire. I'm not sure where 'here' is, exactly, but it's obviously in a mountain of some sort. Much of this food is foreign to me so I'm guessing we're on the mainland, possibly in the Darlangson Mountains?" The last bit came as a question.

"Well done! You have it nearly correct. We're in a smaller range to the west of the Darlangson formation, called the Pywell Mountains. You're quite sharp, I was right about you."

"What did you mean before, about me showing promise for the future?" he asked.

She studied him momentarily. "I think I'll let Zandorn explain that part to you. Are you finished eating? We can go see him presently if you are."

With hesitation, he nodded. He expected he didn't have much choice. Gunther loomed ominously behind Renna looking ready to catch him if he dared run, or defend his mistress from any threat. Kalbick had a feeling she didn't need anyone to defend her, though. The confident stares and dangerous air she carried told Kalbick there was far more to this beautiful girl than he could see.

"Let's get you into something more proper for meeting Zandorn," she said, eyeing his tattered clothes up and down.

Kalbick took a moment to evaluate his own physical status. His pants were thin and torn at the knees. His shirt was ripped from the collar to his midsection, exposing most of his torso. That happened during one of his early fights in the cell when a boy tried to grab his throat and missed. In the daylight he noticed the various bruises and dirt patches that covered most of his body. The smell, which he had become accustomed to, was overpowering when compared to the sweet scents of the food in front of him.

Renna snapped her fingers and his clothes vibrated with magic.

Kalbick looked down and gasped as the garments reworked their stitching, changing from the old linen into the finest silk. As the material moved it slowly faded from stained brown and white into a crimson shirt with black breeches and jacket that cut-off right below his shoulder blades. His new clothing matched Renna's blood-red dress and black robe that was so thin it could have been made from a spider web.

Seemingly content with her work, the two—with Gunther in tow—left the room and made their way to Zandorn's chambers.

"This is it," Renna said outside a large brass door with more carvings than could ever be decipherable.

Kalbick's stomach clenched and turned over, his nerves and the rich feast setting in. Then a surge of fear and shock ran through him. His eyes widened as he whipped around to look at Renna.

"You! You're evil! I mean, you've been kind to me, but why? You and Zandorn, you're, you're—"

Before he could get another word out, Renna placed her hand on his shoulder. "It's all right, Kalbick. You're going to see that soon. You trust me, don't you?"

Kalbick thought he should be screaming *No!* at the top of his lungs, but somehow he suddenly felt calm again. He simply nodded, confused but unable to figure out why.

He watched as Renna turned and placed her palm on the door and closed her eyes. After a moment, the door creaked open slowly.

"Well, are you ready?" she asked as sweetly as ever.

Kalbick gulped, nodded again, and followed the mysterious girl into the room as the door shut behind him.

CHAPTER 9

THE SWIFT STAR

In Zak's dream, an assassin ran through the woods swiftly and silently, like a predator. Zakolor knew he was an assassin by the weapons strapped to his back, the ones that he guessed were hidden, and the way the man carried himself. He stopped next to a flat piece of rock outside a large cave. The rock began glowing and shimmered light blue, as if part of the rock was actually water. A moment later, a dark figure emerged from the rock face. Not just any dark figure, but *the* dark figure, the one that attempted to kidnap Zak. This was Burvenin!

Silverfire and the assassin began conversing. Zakolor strained to hear the words, but it was a futile effort. He was not in control of what was happening. After a few moments, the assassin quickly turned and stared at Zak, looking him right in the eye. He felt a rushing sensation as he was whisked through the countryside back to his room at the inn where he awoke, breathing heavily and drenched in sweat.

His mind raced, sitting up and swinging his legs to touch the floor and bracing himself against the bed, trying to understand what just happened. Before he could begin asking himself questions, there was a knock on his door. He slowly stood and walked the few paces over to open the door.

Sorwin stood there, looking somewhat tired but still smiling. Zak guessed the strain of constantly protecting him was catching up to the Magerus.

"Morning. Everything...okay?" he asked. His eyes darted up and down Zak and quickly around the room, apparently scanning for anything amiss. Zak wondered if he noticed the obvious sweat marks on his clothes and sheets.

"Hi Sorwin. Yeah, I'm fine. Just...some bad dreams," he answered.

Sorwin let a few moments pass silently between them. "Right, well, let's talk about it on the boat. We have to get going, so we'll leave as soon as you're ready." Sorwin nodded and turned, walking downstairs.

Zak hoped he was going to find them some breakfast as he closed the door and wiped his forehead. More tension gripped Zak, and as he packed his things he wondered how to explain his latest experience.

He quickly joined Sorwin downstairs, thanking the mage for the hot breakfast he found waiting. He still wasn't sure if he completely trusted Sorwin, not when he had so many questions left unanswered, but he was grateful the man consistently provided a hot meal. Zak quickly drained the bowl of stew, mopping up the remains with fresh sourdough bread, lightly dusted with extra flour.

The pair left the inn and went directly to the docks. Sorwin explained on the way he had arranged passage on the

Swift Star for them the night before, supposedly one of the fastest ships in the southern seas. Zak recognized the salty breeze of the ocean that brushed his face and knew they found the docks.

Rows and rows of wooden planks, one stacked after the next, stretched out into the water to the floating giants Zak realized were ships. He looked up, his mouth falling open as he admired their sheer size. Stumbling along behind Sorwin, he tried to recall some of the images he had seen in books in school. That was his only experience with ships.

Even though Bernadooth was apparently a small city, it was the main port for all Carshandyn and the smaller isles nearby, and Zak heard as many as twenty ships would arrive or depart on a given day. There were more vessels and docks than he had time to count. Sorwin forged ahead, holding Zak's arm so they wouldn't get separated between the mass of dockworkers, merchants, and passengers.

Eventually Zak saw the words *Swift Star* painted on the side of a medium sized barge, compared to the others floating nearby.

A rotund man lumbered over to them as they approached the ramp leading to the main deck. His sandy-brown hair that was cropped short, bright blue eyes, and rosy cheeks made him look like an oversized child. He flashed a toothy smile at Sorwin and Zak.

"Well, 'ello there Mr. Sorwin! Ye 'bout ready to be castin' off?" his voice boomed.

"Well met, Captain Swortizzle. Yes, just have to load our things on board," Sorwin replied.

"Yer just in time, then, we'll be leavin' any time now!" the captain said. He walked over to stand in front of them. "And who 'ave we 'ere?" he asked the mage.

"This is Zakolor," Sorwin said.

"Pleasure, it is!" Swortizzle offered his hand to Zak. "This is the *Nacusti*, eh?"

Zak flinched slightly, still uncomfortable with the title. "You can call me Zak," he said, shaking Swortizzle's hand.

"Zak it is. Make 'em small nowadays, they do!" He patted Zak on the head before he turned and walked on board, the wood of the ramp bending and creaking under his large mass.

Zak and Sorwin followed Swortizzle up the ramp and onto the main deck. They stopped behind the large captain as he oversaw final preparations for departure.

"We keep 'er well-maintained and clean, ya see. The ship, that is. Same can't be said fer the crew!" he laughed.

Zak couldn't disagree. Many were smeared with dirt and black powder and wafts of wine and whiskey assaulted Zak's nose when a few men walked too close. A few of them smiled as they passed, and Zak had yet to see one with a full set of teeth. They were a rough lot, and he wondered if that was exactly why Sorwin chose this ship.

One of the sailors, a particularly grimy fellow smelling of something sour, led Zak and Sorwin to the guest quarters. He opened the door and held his arm out into the room, bowing as he did so, an awkward and obviously practiced ritual.

Zak and Sorwin nodded politely to the sailor as they passed into the room, and once inside, Sorwin closed the door behind them. They were in a small, plain room with sparse furniture built into the ship. Zakolor claimed one of the four bunk beds while Sorwin placed his things near a wide bed in the middle of the room.

As they settled into their new quarters, Zak must have been more anxious than he realized, as Sorwin said, "I know they seem...different." He searched for the right words to convince Zak of his choice. "But they are the best at what they do, and in our current state, things being what they are, we need the best."

"What exactly do they do?" he asked.

"The *Swift Star* and her crew are mercenaries for hire, accustomed to dangerous expeditions. After sixteen years at sea, the ship, her captain, and crew have established a well-respected reputation."

"Do they know we are being pursued by the Consortium?" Zak asked.

"Yes of course, why wouldn't they?"

"And they still help us? How much are you paying them?"

Sorwin snickered lightly at that. "Many people throughout the realm are willing to help when it comes to the Consortium and the war. If the Consortium won, they would rule Valecium. Fear of their potential triumph overshadows the fear of their immediate threat."

Zak continued unpacking. "I think I saw who was after us," he blurted as he reached into his bag.

Sorwin looked up from the books he was stacking on a nearby desk. "And how were you able to catch a glimpse of them, might I ask?"

"I had another dream," he started, "but this wasn't the same as the other dreams, it felt like I was actually traveling, or living my dream as it happened, not watching the future." Zak was surprised at himself for being so honest, but right now Sorwin was his best option for answers. And he really did seem to have the best intentions so far.

Sorwin thought for a moment before he revealed the answer. "You astral projected," he explained. "Basically, your spirit left your body and traveled on its own. What did you see?"

Zak didn't remember much, and what he did recall was fuzzy at best. After a few moments he said, "A man, standing by a cave, talking to someone..." He considered his words as they fell from his mouth. A sudden revelation cleared some of the fog from his memories. "Burvenin! The man was talking to Burvenin!" he exclaimed.

"Can you remember anything about the man? Any distinct characteristics about him or anything he carried?" Sorwin asked. The mage was speaking faster now.

Again the details of his nighttime excursion escaped him. He shook his head in disappointment.

"Not to worry, whoever he was, he will be hard pressed to strike at us on the open sea while we're under the protection of the *Swift Star*."

Zak remembered one important detail. "There was one more thing. When the man and Burvenin were talking, the man looked right at me as if he could see me, and when he did I went flying back to my real body."

At this, Sorwin's normally relaxed face became tight and

serious. "Did he say anything, a spell, perhaps, when he looked at you?"

"No, he just stared," Zak said.

Sorwin's eyebrows rose, apparently in surprise. It was a look Zak had yet to see on the mage's face. "Few people in the world can send a spirit back to its body without uttering a word," he said. The room was silent and the air felt heavy to Zak. A few moments passed before Sorwin spoke again. "Thank you for bringing this to my attention, Zak. Any information is better than none."

Concerned with the sudden tension that gripped the mage, Zak leaned back in his bunk, opening one of the books Sorwin gave him to resume his studies. His thoughts again drifted to Kal, and his resolve doubled. "I'm coming for you, Kal," he quietly promised again.

Chapter 10

PROXIMITY TO DARKNESS

Kalbick and Renna's footsteps echoed through the great hall. Giant sconces larger than him held flames that gave off an unnatural light. Kalbick thought he should be terrified. Instead, he marveled at his surroundings. The attention to detail the creators of this place had was inspiring. From the epics carved along the walls he was able to deduce the hold was originally dwarven. Ancient battles and kings of old were depicted crushing their enemies or facing persecution for failure. He had heard plenty of stories about the unforgiving civilization of the dwarves, and shuddered at the thought of running into one of the rugged beings.

Even with the magnificent surroundings—definitely the most impressive his young eyes had ever seen—Kalbick's attention was repeatedly drawn back to Renna. Walking a few paces ahead of him, her powerful and determined stride was masked with a regal beauty and ease. There was something about her that Kalbick found interesting and enticing, aside from her obvious physical allure. She had an undeniable confidence and a quality of character he craved to be in the presence of constantly.

At the end of the enormous hall sat an ancient stone throne. Here the carvings culminated in intricacy, some of the details even smaller than the width of a fingernail. They turned left and went down a narrow hallway to what Kalbick guessed was once the old dwarven king's private chambers. Again he thought it odd he wasn't scared, wasn't trying to run the other direction, away from Renna and Zandorn. But he kept moving forward, and he couldn't figure out why.

Pushing open another elaborately designed door, Renna led Kalbick into a medium sized chamber. It was obvious this room was formerly truly spectacular. Beautiful furniture that used to structure the room nicely was pushed against the side walls, abandoned there to collect dust. Ripped oil paintings and tapestries that had been burned or damaged over the years hung on the walls, sad reminders of what once was glorious. Two long tables that looked similar to the one in Renna's chambers stood in front of the stacked furniture, seeming to box all the pieces in. Atop the tables were scattered books, papers with scribbled notes, assorted ingredients, and jars containing objects that were mysteries to Kalbick. As they walked toward the far wall, he could have sworn he saw a few objects on the tables move.

Ahead of him, it didn't take Kalbick long to notice a man chained to the wall. His head hung in exhaustion. Much like the room, the man showed former glory, but was currently in a state of disarray. His finely-woven clothes were dirty and torn, like Kalbick's had been before he met Renna. While there were no visible marks on his body it was easy to see he was broken, more mentally than physically. His face was ashen and a cloud of despair hung over him. This man was another prisoner.

A figure hunched over the end of one of the long tables, scribbling away and murmuring to himself, not bothering to acknowledge Kalbick and Renna's presence. Taking his cue from Renna, Kalbick waited patiently just a step behind his striking captor.

"Hmm, still with us, Ambassador?" the man at the table wondered aloud, turning to the prisoner chained to the wall.

The silkiness of his voice startled Kalbick. He hadn't expected it to be so comforting.

"Does the League know where the Druids are hiding?"

Kalbick watched as the man lifted the ambassador's drooping chin, forcing him to look forward with half open eyes. With his head swaying slightly, the ambassador managed to spit some of the pooling blood from his mouth at the man. Kalbick winced at this, and he wasn't sure why, but he felt a hint of anger toward the ambassador.

"I thought the Royal Darlangson Ambassador would be of more use than this. Pity." And with that the man snapped the ambassador's neck with a twitch of his index finger. The ambassador's head lolled, falling limply to one side. Trickles of blood fell to the floor in long drips.

"Does this mean the hunt for the Druids continues, Father?" Renna queried.

Kalbick stiffened. So this man was Zandorn. He knew he

should be terrified, but he felt paralyzed, like his mind refused to think and his body refused to move. What was happening?

"For now," Zandorn answered.

Finally turning to face his daughter, Kalbick was able to fully take in the man. He was of average height with unnaturally greyish skin. His hair was a deep black like his daughter's, but he possessed none of her beauty. His giant hook nose and angular features made him appear birdlike, almost akin to a carrion. A large, jagged scar started above his right brow and ran down his face, disappearing into the collar of his robes.

"Now, what have you brought me?" he asked, sizing up Kalbick in a similar fashion.

"He has potential to be useful, Father. He passed The Test, and has been very cooperative."

"Has he? Your Influence has nothing to do with that? Release him so we may speak with his will intact."

Renna waved her hand nonchalantly.

Kalbick blinked several times and took a step back. It was like the fog from his mind had been cleared, and he began understanding why he wasn't scared before, why he was cooperating with relative calmness in the presence of his captors.

"You...what did you do to me?" Kalbick asked.

"It's called Influence," Renna explained. "It's magic that bends the subject's will. I can teach you if you'd like."

With the spell abolished Kalbick started panicking. His breathing and heart rate increased and he started sweating. His eyes darted between Renna and Zandorn several times before he made the impulsive decision to turn and run for the door.

"Hmm, yet another disappointment today," Zandorn said.

"Oh please, Father."

Kalbick glanced back and saw Zandorn reached toward him and flick his wrist upward. A wall of stone erupted from the floor to block Kalbick's path. He tried to slow but was running too fast and crashed headlong into the construction. He squirmed on the cold floor, clutching his injured head.

"It's quite a natural response," Renna said, walking towards Kalbick. "Once he acclimates to his circumstances he'll be invaluable."

"What makes you so sure, dearest Daughter?"

"Can you not see it? Look at his magic."

Zandorn crossed the room to Kalbick, wrenched his arms away from his face and lightly tapped his forehead in between his brows.

Kalbick gasped and immediately knew he couldn't move, couldn't control his body. He tried anyway, struggling furiously to punch or scream or kick his way to freedom, but nothing happened. Instead, his body floated a few feet off the ground like he was suspended in water, his body drifting in slow motion. His eyes remained open and fixed on the ceiling, his mouth agape. Kalbick saw Zandorn close his eyes. His face worked through various expressions before landing on what Kalbick guessed was surprise.

"His magic is—" he started.

"Yes," Renna responded.

"Is it sustainable?"

"That's what I want to find out."

Zandorn opened his eyes again and stared directly into Kalbick's. "Curious," he whispered, releasing Kalbick from his static state. He fell hard to the floor, wincing when he landed.

"He is your charge now, Renna. Train him, educate him, and bring him to me once a week. I will need to study his progress."

"Yes, Father," she said, bowing slightly. She snapped her fingers and Gunther lumbered through the door, dipping his head to fit through the door frame. He gently picked up Kalbick and followed Renna out. Within a few strides down the hallway, Kalbick blacked out.

CHAPTER 11
WEAPONS

S orwin stood a few yards away from Zak on the main deck of the *Swift Star*, the two facing each other.

"You have impressed me over the last few weeks, Zakolor. You are using spells regularly and intentionally, and your meditation is coming along rather well."

Thinking back to Zak's description of the man by the rock from his "dream," Sorwin considered his next course of tutelage.

"Magic is a mage's best weapon and defense, but there will come a time when magic will not be enough or will be absent altogether, and you will have to rely on other skills to survive."

Zakolor's face scrunched, apparently in confusion. Sorwin continued.

"As you've realized, using magic tires out the mage. Your power can grow and be restored through practice and meditation, but someday you will find yourself drained and without the time to rest. That is why it is imperative that you learn to wield a weapon."

Zak seemed a little surprised. "You mean, you can teach me? I know you carry a sword and figured you must know how to use it, but you're going to teach me that instead of magic?"

"Why do you assume 'instead of magic'? Why can't I do both?" A wry smile crossed his face.

"Well, it's not that you can't. I just thought—"

"Good! Then we'll do both. You'd agree that is the most likely scenario to help you find Kalbick, correct? Learning magic and combat?" Sorwin didn't like the idea of using this angle to pressure Zak, but he needed the boy to focus, to be motivated. He had so much to learn in so little time.

It had the desired effect, and Zak's demeanor shifted significantly at the mention of Kalbick. He unconsciously widened his stance and steeled his jaw, nodding once with determination.

"First," Sorwin said, "I will teach you how to summon a sparring weapon. They are much safer than real weapons because they are pure, magical energy. At most they will leave a large bruise, but they replicate the exact weight and feel of normal weapons."

He taught Zak the incantation and physical maneuvers required for the spell. Within minutes, Zak was holding a six foot mahogany staff with an emerald in the tip and looking very confused.

"Why did you teach me how to summon a staff instead of a sword?" Zak asked, glancing at Sorwin's steel blade, the orange gemstones adorning the hilt.

"We don't get to choose the weapons of our soul, Zak,"

he said. "You were meant to wield a staff, so that is what you conjured."

Zak shrugged and looked at his weapon. It was smooth, beautiful, and hard as any metal. He looked at the emerald on the end of his staff and shot another questioning look at Sorwin.

He caught the unspoken question. "When you conjure something of pure magic, some of your magic leaves its mark, and every mark is as individual as our personalities." As he finished, he pointed to the orange that was displayed on the hilt of his sword. Apparently satisfied, Zak steadied himself on the shifting deck of the ship, ready for his first lesson in combat.

Sorwin walked him through a series of parries and blocks, teaching him the correct technique as they went. He learned how to stop attacks from all angles and how to disarm his foe. By the end of the first session, Zak was drenched and had earned a few bruises.

"Well done," Sorwin said as they dismissed their sparring weapons with a snap of their fingers. "Far better than I did in my first bout."

Zak smiled, pleased with the praise. It was brief and quickly replaced with the usual shadow on his face.

Sorwin guessed this was the weight of responsibility he felt for finding his lost friend.

"I think that's all for now. Rest and meditate. Then we'll review some reading and spells before dinner."

"Yes, Sorwin," Zak replied.

Zak ladled some water out of a nearby bucket, drinking the first spoonful then dumping another over his head, washing some of the sweat away from his sparring lesson.

He shook the darker thoughts of Kalbick's situation from his head and tried to enjoy as much of his current experience as he could. He was on a ship for the first time, in the middle of the sea! When would this happen again, if ever?

Maybe on the way home to Densba, he thought. If he managed to survive long enough to return.

Zak wandered up to the helm and found Swortizzle guiding the ship with ease.

"Afternoon to yuh, young Acolyte Zak," he boomed. The man was so large and had so much enthusiasm Zakolor thought it was impossible for him to be any quieter.

"Afternoon, Captain," he answered. "What's an Acolyte?"

"Oh! I though' Mr. Sorwin woulda told yuh. Tha's the name o' beginner mages, it is."

"I see," Zak said. "How're the winds today?"

"They be blowin' a fair direction today, me boy. A right fair direction." After a brief pause, the captain noticed something on deck that made him smile. "Well, lookah here, me boy. Looks like little Momo is havin' fun with Creagan!"

Zak followed the line of the captain's finger pointing to the far end of the main deck, opposite the helm. Momo, the captain's playful parrot, was swooping at Creagan, the crewmember who had shown them to their chambers a few days ago. He was defending his meal from the bird with an ornery expression. It was obvious the sailor's short temper was quickly being exhausted. He swung one arm warningly at the bird when it dove too close.

"Dangit, Captain, get yer bird under control! It'll eat me fingers afore it gets me bread!" Creagan yelled, still swinging all the while.

Swortizzle laughed heartily, enjoying the spectacle. "He's just keepin' yuh on yer toes, Creag. The exercise will do yuh good!"

Momo dove again and actually did manage to bite one of Creagan's fingers on a wild swing of his arm. The man yelped and pulled his injured hand close to his chest while the bird fluttered above him, squawking with pride.

"That's it! He's gettin' it now!" Creagan yelled, drawing his sword and chasing after the mischievous parrot.

The scene gathered the attention of the entire crew, and now all of them were laughing and mocking Creagan, throwing out smart remarks at leisure. Creagan ignored most of them, muttering curses to the parrot under his breath as he chased the bird and swung his sword. Momo led him too close to the mainmast. On one of Creagan's furious sword swipes he accidentally lodged his blade in the mainmast, cutting several ropes attached to the mainsail in the process. The lines whipped up the mast at a speed almost too fast to see. Creagan looked up, his anger replaced with astonishment and fear.

Momo flew to the captain's shoulder and landed, squawking, "Uh-oh, trouble trouble!"

Momo was right. The lines that were cut had such a violent ascent they cut and tangled others and broke several pulleys.

A few crew scrambled to grab some of the ropes before they flew up and out of reach. They were too slow, and the one rope they managed to contain proved quite challenging for three men.

Zak scanned the deck quickly but couldn't find Sorwin anywhere. *He must be below deck*, he thought. More snapping and breaking sounds came from the top of the mast, and suddenly the entire mainsail was on its way down.

The men below tried to scramble out of the way, but all the fallen rope and debris hindered them. They wouldn't make it in time. They would be crushed under the mast.

Zak yanked off his jade necklace, reached for his magic, pulled as much as he could, thrust his palm toward the falling sail, and yelled, "Relentesco!"

The sail immediately halted, or seemed to. It was, in fact, moving so slowly that it was barely perceptible. The sail hovered above the men, less than a foot from their cringing faces.

Sustaining the spell was a massive effort for Zak. He fell to his knees, keeping his hand outstretched. He used his other hand to support his arm. It felt like someone dropped bars of iron on it, like the ones his father taught him how to work with at the smithy. He knew he couldn't drop his arm, otherwise the spell would be released, leaving the sail to fall and crush the crew.

Sorwin was in his room planning the route to Tor'alan once they made land. Suddenly, a series of loud crashes and yelling from the deck broke his concentration.

"Zakolor," he said to himself, leaping out the door and sprinting up the narrow stairs to the main deck. When he got there, he saw a dozen ropes, pulleys, and the mainsail suspended in midair above half the crew as they tried to scramble out from beneath the debris.

Sorwin looked across the deck and saw Zak kneeling with his arm outstretched toward the sail. Even from across the deck he could see the boy's eyes were glowing a bright green. Without hesitating, Sorwin ran toward Zak, slowing as he approached.

The spell gave the men enough time to escape the descending mass, and everyone was safe. Yet Zak wasn't releasing the spell.

"Zak," Sorwin said, slowly walking toward the boy. "You can let go now. Everyone is safe."

Zak's face twinged in what looked like pain. "I can't," he grunted between gritted teeth.

"Why?"

"I can't," he repeated.

"Tell me why, Zak."

"Because I don't want to!" His head snapped toward Sorwin as he yelled, his voice deepened and his eyes flared a brighter green. He snarled and growled like a wild animal defending a kill.

"What's wrong with 'im, Magerus?" Swortizzle asked, stepping up behind Sorwin.

"He's not himself right now," Sorwin said, still slowly approaching. He reached inside his robe and pulled out a small leather purse.

"Oh aye, that I can see. Jus' who he bein' yuh suppose?"

From the leather purse, Sorwin pulled a palm-sized jewel with an impossible number of colors streaking through it.

When Zak saw it he snarled defensively. His eyes followed it as Sorwin continued to get closer and closer.

"I'm just going to have you hold this for me for a moment, Zak," Sorwin said calmly, reaching out toward Zak. He gently pressed the jewel into Zak's outstretched palm.

Zak resisted initially, but curiosity seemed to win out and the boy instinctively grabbed it. He held it for a moment, examining the stone before his eyes closed and he lost consciousness.

As he fell forward, Sorwin leaned in, catching him and the jewel simultaneously before either hit the deck.

The sail landed with a solid thud below, and everyone jumped with the sudden movement as Zak's spell broke.

"Is everyone all right?" Sorwin yelled, loud enough for the crew to hear. He replaced the stone in the leather purse and studied his young apprentice, looking for injuries.

Gaining his bearings, the captain managed a reply. "We be fine now, mage, thanks to yer Acolyte 'ere. Yuh reckon he will be too?"

Sorwin recognized more than a bit of concern in the

captain's voice, realizing he had become quite fond of Zak in a remarkably short time.

"He will be after some rest," Sorwin said.

Swortizzle nodded and called over a few crew members to help carry Zak below deck to his bed.

Zak sat bolt upright, breathing heavily, and looked around the room, confused. Sorwin was by his side in an instant.

"How do you feel?" Sorwin asked.

His breathing slowed to a normal pace. "Fine," he answered. "My head is killing me, and I feel tired, but I'm okay. What happened?"

"What do you remember?"

Zak thought for a moment. "I remember Momo and Creagan and the sail falling—oh Cerevita, is everyone okay?"

"They're fine, thanks to you," Sorwin said, a smile crossing his face for a second. It was quickly replaced with what Zak knew to be concern. "What else do you remember?"

"I cast a spell, the slowing spell, to give the crew time to move. After that, nothing." A few beats passed. "What happened? Did I pass out?"

He could see Sorwin hesitate for a moment, as if debating what to say. The muscles on his jawline tensed.

"Yes," he said finally. "The strain was too much when you didn't release the spell. Try and let go sooner next time, hmm?" He handed Zak a wooden cup with water and turned back to his books and papers, shuffling them into some sort of order.

"Yes, Sorwin," Zak answered. His eyes lingered on the mage for a few moments. He couldn't help but feel there was something else he didn't know.

CHAPTER 12
THE VOID

Zak watched from the main deck as Captain Swortizzle gently guided the *Swift Star* into Lindomer with an easy expertise. The ship dropped anchor and finally groaned to a slow halt at one of the last docks. To Zak, it almost felt as if the ship was tired and happy to have a rest. The crew quickly began unloading other shipments they had been commissioned to carry.

He felt more sad than he expected to say goodbye to the ship and her crew. Over the last week he had grown fond of them, and he thought they felt the same towards him. He had his proof the night before when some of the crew said their goodbyes in advance, knowing there would be no time this morning. It was a sad affair, for all that they were tough, sea-hardened, salty mercenaries, they were still people. Many cried without shame.

"Well, ye be makin' sure yer not fergettin' us down 'ere by the coast, ye hear?" Captain Swortizzle said, waddling over to stand in front of Zak. "If ever ye be needin' safe passage on the sea ye don't be thinkin' 'bout callin' nobody but me!"

Zak smiled. "I wouldn't dare, Captain. I can't thank you enough for keeping us safe, and getting us here so fast."

"It's true, we owe you more than we can pay," Sorwin said, joining the farewell.

"Ah, it's nothin' yer wouldn'ta done fer me," the captain replied. His face changed to a more serious look, an odd expression for his normally jovial face. "Jus' be takin' care o' yerselves, right? Straight to Tor'alan with yer?"

"All we need is two good horses and we'll be on our way," Sorwin confirmed.

"If yer head straight ter the north gate, ask fer Giacomo. He's got ter best steeds yer ever done seen."

"Many thanks, Captain, we'll do just that." Sorwin braced arms with Swortizzle.

The captain nodded again, his eyes lingering on Zak with an expression that looked to be a mixture of hope and fear. Zak offered a weak smile before turning and grabbing his bag and following Sorwin down the walkway to the dock.

Zak immediately felt strange. "Oh!" He stumbled and ran into Sorwin, pushing the mage forward an extra step. "Sorry," he apologized as he regained his balance.

"Quite fine, not to worry," Sorwin said. "I forgot to mention the adjustment period between sea and land. You should be fine in a few minutes."

Sorwin explained that his body had become accustomed to the swaying of waves and currents. Now, he swayed back and forth a little as his body continued adjusting for a motion that was now absent.

Zak leaned on Sorwin as the mage led him through the

rows of docks and into the city. Lindomer was one of the largest cities in the League, second only to Tor'alan. Zak remembered from school that the city boasted a strong economy and rather prestigious academies. He marveled at the beautiful and ancient architecture of the city. His island home was old as well, but new for human inhabitants, having been settled almost three hundred years ago. It was obvious that these soaring structures were far older than that.

Once in the city proper, Zak sensed something wrong. He had never been to Lindomer and had no idea what the city was normally like, but he had a feeling something was off. It took him several minutes to figure out why. The streets bustled with business, he saw a number of poor and beggar-type, which he thought was probably normal for a city this size. City guards patrolled in pairs and didn't seem overly alert or concerned. He was about to brush off his feeling when he saw the first mark.

It was ahead and to their right—a large, black mark that stretched from the bottom of a tree into the middle of the trunk, as if it was slowly climbing. As Zak moved closer, he smelled the unique scent anyone from a small farm community would know: death.

"What is that?" Zak asked, pointing to the mark on the tree.

Sorwin's eyes narrowed. "It's reached this far south already." He sighed, looking at the tree with the mark. "That is the Rot, a result of Zandorn's dark magic. You see, magic is in all things, and his perversion of magic and life itself through necromancy has a cost. The world is dying, Zakolor. This is evidence of that fact. I thought we had more time, but it seems to be spreading quickly."

"Spreading? From where?"

"From the north, where Zandorn was originally conducting his experiments. He's moved now, but the decay continues to spread from that original spot. There are many reasons we need to stop Zandorn, but this is the most immediate. If he continues, or if he succeeds, we will all die."

"And I'm the only one who can stop him?" Zak asked. He knew the answer, but he wanted to keep Sorwin talking, hoping to get more information from him.

"Yes," Sorwin said. His eyes stared down at the path in front of them as they continued their march through the city.

Zak knew Sorwin well enough now to be worried whenever he used few words. Sorwin was a man who was excited about teaching, learning, and enlightening. If he withheld information, Zak assumed it was reserved for the most serious and dangerous of reasons.

He tried with difficulty to inhale for several seconds, the metaphoric gravity of his responsibility felt suddenly literal on his chest. Instead of information, Zak only found more fear, more pressure, more responsibility. It was enough to make him stop asking questions for the moment.

Within an hour Zak and Sorwin made it to Giacomo's, haggled for horses, and were on the road to Tor'alan.

"Stay close and move fast," Sorwin instructed. "It's a week's ride to Tor'alan and we don't know what Zandorn and the Consortium are prepared to try on us."

Zak nodded and coaxed his pale yellow horse into a quick

canter behind Sorwin.

It was a melancholy day. Heavy clouds threatened the earth with rain. Zakolor watched several wild animals, ranging from birds to deer to stray cats, take cover from the imminent downpour as he bumped along on the back of his horse. It had been another hard week on the road since they left Lindomer.

Sorwin took every precaution with his wards and used a fair amount of energy on detection spells when he could. His efforts seemed to have paid off as they hadn't encountered a single Consortium agent.

Ahead was the strangest sight Zak had seen in his young life. He pulled his horse to a stop to observe it.

There was really no way to describe it, it was simply a floating city.

Suspended in the air—by what Zak guessed was extremely powerful magic—was a magnificent metropolis, glittering in rays of sunlight blasting through the clouds almost a mile away.

"The League's capital, Tor'alan," Sorwin said.

Zak was in awe of the spectacle. He even felt a little hope for himself and for Kalbick. If the League was capable of this incredible feat, of suspending an entire *city* in the air, surely they could defeat Zandorn. Surely they could find his lost friend. *They must be able to help*, he thought. Zak needed them to be able to help.

"This is where your future truly begins, Zakolor." Sorwin said, nudging his horse forward and down the winding path.

He followed, feeling a mixture of fear, excitement, and hope. Trotting toward the looming city was unexpectedly overwhelming. He wanted to distract himself, to focus on something to ease the assault of emotions. He decided to practice one of the tactics Sorwin started teaching him over the last week: observation.

Sorwin had said that observation could be a powerful tool for anyone, and could even be the difference between life and death in perilous situations. Noticing weaknesses, or escape opportunities, or subtle differences or changes in the environment that could precede an ambush.

Zak agreed with his teacher's mentality, plus he enjoyed the exercise of trying to observe as many things as possible. He had never enjoyed or excelled at learning through books, but he loved the "learn by doing" approach.

He started with the road. A wide, dirt road led to Tor'alan. It seemed normal, many foot and hoof prints and wagon wheel tracks were evident. Zak counted close to two dozen people within eyesight. Two guards walked slowly up and down the road ahead. He turned around: another five people behind him. Two heading the same direction as him, three in the opposite. He faced forward again. Two birds flitted and chased one another off to the right. By the side of the road he saw an array of debris: apple cores, broken wheels, and other apparently useless gear and items. When he was about to move on to the hedgerow to his right, he heard a loud shriek to his left.

Two giant shadoweres bound out of the woods toward him and Sorwin.

Zak gasped sharply. *No*, he thought. *It's happening again, just like before. The Consortium found them!*

The beasts were closing the gap to Zak and Sorwin in seconds. People everywhere scattered, running in the opposite direction.

Sorwin waved his hand and forced one of the beasts to crash into the other, causing them both to tumble. "Go! Ride as quickly as you can for the city!" he yelled to Zak. The mage was already dismounting and preparing another spell.

"Wait, I can help!" Zak yelled back. He was sweating, afraid, and vibrating with nervous energy, but he knew if he couldn't face these two beasts now he didn't have a chance of finding and saving Kalbick. This was something he needed to do.

As he steeled his resolve, motion near the trees caught his attention. Five men dressed in black with dark blue hoods came running out of the woods toward Sorwin, each of them brandishing a different weapon.

Zak jumped down from his horse and was about to rush in to help when he saw a large spear flying through the air to his right. It hit a wagon a few yards ahead of him, splintering one of the wheels on impact. The wagon slid to a stop, throwing a man to the ground in the process. He looked to be getting his bearings when a woman and two children climbed out of the back of the wagon.

Further ahead Zak saw three more men dressed in the same black and blue uniforms. One had a bow and arrow, one a large battleaxe, and the third drew a longsword from a scabbard. The last two approached at a slow trot while the archer began firing arrows at the wagon.

Without a thought Zak ran toward the wagon. He could see the Tor'alan guards sprinting toward the wagon as well, but they'd never make it in time to save the family. The woman had come around to the front of the wagon and was helping the man to his feet when an arrow lodged itself into the seat next to her head.

A second arrow pierced the air, nicking the man's upper arm. He yelped in pain, grabbing his arm and trying to hurry to cover, but he and the woman fell in their haste.

Zak skidded to a stop in front of them, held his hand above his head and yelled "*Tegoperignis!*"

Green fire flowed down from his hand, circling him and the man and woman as they crouched on the ground behind him. Three more arrows flew in their direction but incinerated upon contact with the shield. His weeks of practice had paid off, the surface of his shield was far smoother and flared less. He held the defense, energy pouring from him as the other two mercenaries approached.

Sorwin had but a second to register Zak's predicament before dealing with his own. Both shadoweres were shaking off the last rebuff and the group of mercenaries was nearly upon him. He closed his eyes for a second, calmed his breathing, found his center, and launched into action.

He used both hands to shoot concentrated streams of fire at the first shadowere. It howled painfully and erupted into a cloud of smoke. A mercenary came in on his right, swinging a sword wildly. Sorwin caught his arm by the wrist, disarmed him with a blow from his knee and threw the man to the ground. He turned, drew his own sword, and met another attack aimed for his torso. He parried the blade several times before shifting into the astral plane and disappearing in a wisp of smoke, dodging a diving shadowere that would have bitten him in half. Sorwin reappeared several yards behind his attackers and leveled his sword towards them. A bolt of lightning came out of the blade and ripped through the air into the mercenary's back, careening him into the shadowere.

Flicking his wrist, he sent the disarmed man's sword flying into another adversary. He lifted his left hand, causing a solid column of rock to rise in the path of an advancing mercenary. The man ran straight into it and lost consciousness before hitting the ground.

The shadowere was up again. Sorwin parried teeth and claws with his sword, backpedaling to stay out from underneath the beast. He ducked below a sideswipe from his right and rounded the beast, thrusting his sword into its side. It yelped briefly, having its lungs pierced, before dissipating into black smoke. The last two mercenaries ran towards him. He held out his hand and said *"Dormio."* The men fell asleep mid-stride and tumbled to the ground.

As Sorwin turned to look toward Zak he barely pulled his sword up in time to meet a quickly descending blade.

"Now, now, you still have me to deal with," said a man

with a venomous smile. He had a small frame and a second sword strapped to his back.

"Who are you?" Sorwin asked.

"I'm hurt you don't know me, Hawk mage," the man answered. "I know your reputation quite well."

Sorwin pushed against the man's sword and broke their connection, taking several steps back to give himself space. This man seemed far more dangerous and capable than the other mercenaries.

"Let's even the odds then, shall we?" Sorwin said. "Who are you?" he repeated.

The man smiled again. "I am Karazul, and the odds are *far* from even."

Zak held his shield while the mercenaries with the axe and sword rained heavy blows upon it, causing him to wince and stagger. The wagon had caught fire due to the shield's close proximity. Another solid blow from the battleaxe sent Zak to the ground, breaking his spell.

The axe had glanced off the shield and lodged itself into the side of the blazing wagon. The wielder worked to free it as the swordsman advanced on Zak.

He bought enough time for the Tor'alan guards to arrive. They split, one taking the axe wielder and one lunging in to stop the sword wielder's advance on Zak and the family behind him.

Zak stood just in time to see the archer fire another arrow.

He managed to send it flying harmlessly aside with a wave of his hand. He did this with another two arrows, realizing he needed a plan. With the third arrow he yelled *"Relentesco!"* The arrow slowed nearly to a halt in midair, giving Zak time to flip its direction and send it back the way it came with his telekinesis. It zipped back and straight into the archer's right shoulder, sending him to the ground.

The axeman bashed his weapon against the Tor'alan guard's helmet, knocking him out, then charged toward Zak.

He dodged several swings since the weapon was large and cumbersome and he was smaller and lithe. He knew he couldn't keep it up forever though.

The axeman caught him off balance and pushed him with the shaft of the axe.

Zak flew backwards and hit the ground hard, gasping for air. He waved his hand and caused the man's foot to fly sideways mid-step. He fell to the ground as the large blade of his axe pierced his torso upon landing. Zak saw the other guard jamming the hilt of his sword into the mercenary's face. The man fell, unconscious.

Still sprawled on the ground, Zak looked at the vacant eyes of the axeman. It was the first time he had taken a life. It wasn't intentional, but it happened. *He* did it. He couldn't tell how he felt. Sad, he knew. Also shock—he expected to be in battle eventually, but he didn't imagine how he would feel if he took a life. Adrenaline flooded his veins during the fight. He felt the buzzing energy clouding his emotions.

"Thank you," said the man. He approached Zak and shook his hand, tears spilling down his cheeks in watery streaks. The woman was close behind, throwing her arms around Zak in a big hug.

Seeing that the family was safe, Zak knew he did what he had to do.

He checked on the other guard before he spotted Sorwin, locked in combat with a single man. If one man forced Sorwin to a standstill, he must be incredibly dangerous.

Maybe that's our pursuer, he thought. Zak took off running to help his magus.

Karazul's blades whipped in silver flashes. It was all Sorwin could do to keep parrying the blows. While he was an accomplished swordsman, his strength lay in the magical arts, and this man was in a martial class all his own.

Finally Sorwin created a small gap. He pushed with all his telekinetic might toward the man. Astonishingly, Karazul only took a few steps backwards. He should have flown nearly thirty feet.

"Is that really it?" Karazul said, still smiling. He launched another blinding flurry of attacks.

Why didn't that work? Sorwin continued to lose ground, thinking of his next strategy while trying to stay alive. A blade nicked his left shoulder, drawing a thin line of blood. He needed time. He shifted again in a wisp of smoke, heading to the astral plane.

"No you don't!" Karazul launched himself forward, dropped the sword in his left hand and grabbed at the air.

Upon contact, Sorwin came back to the physical plane with Karazul's hand latched around his throat.

How had he done that? Unless, could this man be...

"You, you're the Void," Sorwin whispered hoarsely, the dangerous man still clutching his throat.

"Ah, very good! I'm quite flattered you've heard of me," Karazul said. "Unfortunately I've been tasked to kill you, so the realization is a little too late."

Sorwin reached for his magic, but it was blocked. He couldn't cast a spell!

Apparently Karazul felt his effort. "Now, none of that, I'm afraid. You know who I am, so I assume you know how this works. I am the Void, the antimagic. My touch renders you powerless."

"That is unfortunate," Sorwin said, and a slight smile appeared on his face. "However, your power has its limits."

"Does it?" Karazul tightened his grip on Sorwin's throat. His eyes glinted, perhaps with curiosity. "Do explain."

Sorwin coughed, knowing he only needed a few more seconds. "Well, for one thing, it hasn't rendered me apprentice-less," he said.

Karazul quickly turned, but he was too late. Hundreds of small leaf darts flew towards him. Four buried themselves in his back before he was able to fully turn. He dropped Sorwin's throat and rolled to the ground and picked up his other blade in one fluid motion. The assassin began parrying and slicing the leaves, not letting another dart touch him.

The distraction worked perfectly, giving Sorwin enough time to put a good distance between him and Karazul. He ran to Zakolor's side and patted his shoulder in appreciation.

"Your timing is really something," Sorwin said, smiling what Zak thought was his first genuine smile in weeks.

Zak returned the smile. "I learned from the best," he said.

He was flooded with relief to have Sorwin next to him again. He felt safe, and what mistrust he had left for the mage largely evaporated during the battle. If Sorwin was willing to risk his life for weeks to protect him from such attacks, Zak thought he must be telling the truth about everything.

Sorwin patted him again and turned as they squared off against the man together.

After the last leaf was destroyed, the man evaluated his surroundings, looking over the various bodies and destruction and back to Sorwin and Zak.

"I enjoyed this thoroughly," he stated, an unnerving smile on his face.

He sheathed his swords, reached into his shirt and pulled out a medallion that hung around his neck. He held it in both hands, closed his eyes and whispered something Zak couldn't hear. The man shifted and disappeared into a wisp of smoke.

"Where did he go?" Zak asked, eyes darting as if the man would reappear at any moment.

"Far away. That was a long-range teleportation spell," Sorwin said.

"I've seen him before, that night I astral projected. He was the man with Burvenin."

"I'm not surprised. He's called the Void, an assassin spe-cializing in killing mages. His is a unique gift, he can absorb and block magic. No one is quite sure where it goes or how it works, hence his namesake. He is one of the few people capable of sending your spirit back to your body without saying a word."

Zak shuddered. Between the Void and Burvenin, saving Kalbick was getting more and more challenging.

In the aftermath of the skirmish, at least three mercenar-ies lay dead. The wagon was in full blaze now, and the guard was restraining the few mercenaries that survived the attack. Further down the road Zak saw a squad of guards sprinting towards them. They must have seen the commotion from the city or a nearby outpost.

Most of the other people on the road escaped the fight, but Sorwin walked through the few groups of civilians that remained, healing minor injuries and accepting thanks. Zak, to his surprise, also received numerous thanks and apprecia-tive pats. This was all so foreign to him. He didn't feel like he did anything besides react to a situation.

Once the guards arrived and seemed to have everything under control, Zak and Sorwin found their horses and rode the last little stretch of the long trek to Tor'alan.

CHAPTER 13
BELCOUR BLOOD

Zak's disbelief and amazement increased the closer he drew to Tor'alan. The shadow of the massive city covered the land for miles. The bottom of the floating island was raw, jagged earth that stretched down toward the ground.

"It's spelled to hold its shape and resist deterioration," Sorwin explained.

"It's fantastic." Zak smiled. Despite all of the danger it had brought him so far, he truly loved magic.

They dismounted and handed the reins of their horses to a young attendant working a nearby makeshift stable. Zak guessed they must migrate it with the city as it moved throughout the countryside.

He followed Sorwin under the floating city, walking to the middle, the lowest point. A single, long spire of stone twisted down towards them. Flattening out at the end, the center was smooth quartz with dark black lines painting a hawk grasping an apple and a rose. Quartz tendrils fanned out around the picture.

"What is that?" Zak asked.

"My family seal," Sorwin said. "The foundation for the city came from the mountain range of my home, and the city founders chose to honor our gift with this seal at the entrance to the city. The hawk is our familiar, the apple represents knowledge and ambition, and the rose reminds us to rule with love so that we may be worthy of our authority and responsibility and never lose our path. Now, shall we continue on *our* path?"

Sorwin pulled Zak close as they both looked up at the sigil. He spoke words Zak could not comprehend and ended with both of their names.

A swirling sensation turned his stomach as flashes of hundreds of images whipped by his face. Instantly, he was standing on a raised dais, gasping for breath.

"Ah, your first portal was a success," Sorwin said, smiling.

Zak lurched forward, hands on his knees, not confident about keeping his last meal down.

"Oh yes, there's that part as well. It gets much easier, I promise." Sorwin sounded a little apologetic.

"Where to...first?" Zak asked through gritted teeth.

"To the Center." Sorwin pointed toward a large tower that appeared in the middle of the floating city. It was far taller than any other structure.

He nodded and followed as Sorwin set off at a quick pace, no doubt eager to share the news of their arrival and the Void's involvement with the Consortium.

Zak surmised they had arrived in the city's market district. Shops lined the streets selling a myriad of wares, vendors shouted advertisements for their goods, customers haggled, and League Marks clinked between palms.

The city—or at least this district—was planned down to the inch. There were no winding streets like in Lindomer or Bernadooth. These streets were an organized grid and incredibly clean, Zak noticed. Most of the buildings were three stories tall and made of a light colored stone, creams and whites and light browns melded together or stood apart. Rooftops varied in shape and color from dark blues to vibrant yellows and reds.

As they walked along, Zak heard—and then saw—a short, angry man yelling at a vendor.

"This is absurd! How *dare* you charge me when you owe me three months' rent! I should have you evicted on the spot. Go, start packing your things."

"No, please! Mr. Euphemius, I beg of you, take whatever you like! I promise I'll get you the Marks soon! Please just let me and my family stay here," pleaded the man.

"What seems to be the problem?" Sorwin asked, coming to a halt next to the vendor's stand. "Ah, Euphemius, patronizing locals again?"

The man who was yelling, apparently Euphemius, spun on his heel to face Sorwin. He was incredibly short, the top of his head reaching no more than a few inches below Zak's shoulder. He wore a large hat, possibly to give him the appearance of a taller stature, but it had the opposite effect. He was just past middle-aged and obviously wealthy. His clothes were made of fine silks that were perfectly tailored. A well-groomed salt-and-pepper mustache sat stubbornly on his upper lip.

Behind Euphemius' right shoulder lurched a tall, round man who was his opposite in every way. On his left stood a young girl who appeared to be around Zak's age. Her auburn hair fell in cascading waves around her face. She wore a red and silver uniform with a short sword strapped to her waist. Her eyes quickly scanned Zak before focusing on Sorwin.

"This doesn't concern you, mage," Euphemius grunted. "This is a personal matter."

"Now, Euphemius, let's not be rude. I'm sure an agreement can be made." Sorwin used one of his more charming smiles.

Zak wondered if he was strictly being cordial or if a hint of spite crept into the curl of his lips.

"Couldn't you give this hardworking gentleman another month to pay his rent? Consider it a favor to me. I do believe you owe me for adding this fine mage to your services." Sorwin gestured to the auburn-haired girl.

Euphemius paused for a moment, frustration building in his brow as he reddened. His eyes narrowed and was clearly unhappy with Sorwin when saying: "Fine, but I'll be back for you," he said, attempting to point menacingly at the vendor.

He had to point so high because of his height that the intimidation factor was lost. He turned quickly and walked away. His bodyguard and the young girl followed. She turned to look back at Zak as she did.

"Who was that?" Zak asked. He realized this question was becoming far too common.

"Euphemius Van Illia. He has quite a chip on his shoulder. He is the illegitimate son of a count in an eastern kingdom. His desire to be legitimate has molded him into a financial giant. Euphemius thinks he can buy his way into nobility, where he believes he already belongs. He is obsessed with power, status, and material things. He has done well for himself. He's one of the wealthiest private benefactors contributing to the war effort," Sorwin explained.

"I meant to ask who the girl was," Zak said, blushing slightly.

"Ah, yes. That was Olivia. She's a second-year mage. I matched her with Euphemius a few months ago. She needed a sponsor for her studies, you see, she's an orphan. With his particular desires, I knew he couldn't refuse the chance to sponsor a rarity such as her."

"What makes her a rarity?" Zak asked almost immediately.

"She can fuse elements quicker than anyone I've seen. It's an advanced magic, usually taking years to master one fusion. She's already completed two fusions in as many years."

"And a fusion is..." Zak started, leading his mentor to fill in the blank.

Sorwin's eyes lit up at the chance to share more knowledge. He gestured for them to keep walking as he spoke.

"You know from your studies thus far there are four basic elements: fire, earth, water, and air. It's possible to fuse the elements together to create new ones as well. Take lightning for instance, that is a fusion of air and fire."

Zak nodded his understanding. He had already seen Sorwin use lightning several times. It was devastating magic.

"So Euphemius has the prestige of a talented mage following him around, and in return Olivia gets what, exactly?" Zak asked.

"In return for serving as his personal bodyguard and liaison, she receives funding for her education and living expenses. It's not quite as common practice these days, but it's still done on occasion."

"So she's bound to him?"

Sorwin frowned. "In a manner of speaking. I can delve into the details later if you wish. Right now, we must get to the Center. Archmagus Tansil will want to see you immediately."

Zak's stomach clenched, not unlike when he went through the portal a few minutes before. He was nervous to meet Tansil, the leader of the League's elemental mages.

Sorwin hadn't divulged much about him over the weeks of his traveling tutelage. He knew Tansil was an elf and one of the most accomplished mages to walk Valecium. Sorwin spoke highly of him, but Zak thought Sorwin would speak highly of anyone with immense amounts of knowledge in their heads.

Zak and Sorwin quickly covered the remaining distance to the Center. It was a massive castle surrounded by a circular wall. Inside the wall was an expanse of grounds with several smaller buildings dotting the yard, meant for housing, lessons, and various other functions. The light-colored stone was a similar hue to the buildings in the market district, yet this stone had swirls of orange and purple mixed in, making the structure almost glow in the sunlight.

Sorwin moved through the castle so quickly that Zak

had little chance to take in the place. It was cold, drafty, yet exquisite. Ornate decorations and details were in every nook and cranny. Their footsteps echoed as he hurried behind the mage. Finally, at the top of a spiral staircase, they came to a pair of large wooden doors banded with iron. Sorwin pushed right through the door without slowing and led him into a large windowed room. Zak guessed they must be in one of the castle spires due to the number of windows circling the room.

In front of him, behind a large mahogany desk, sat a man unlike Zak had ever seen before. Bright green eyes looked up from a mess of papers and directly at him as he and Sorwin stopped a few feet away. Zak was startled by the intensity of those eyes. They glowed just as bright as the numerous candles lighting the room. Zak couldn't help but wonder if the creature even needed the candles to see with eyes that bright.

"Tansil, this is Zakolor Keldin," Sorwin's voice cut into Zak's thoughts. "Zakolor, this is the Archmagus Tansil Windover, Head of the Elemental House and Bearer of the Heart of Life."

Zak wasn't sure what to do, Sorwin hadn't explained anything about actually meeting Tansil. He awkwardly nodded and half-bowed.

"It's nice to meet you, Archmagus," he managed to say, his voice trembling more than he liked.

"*Benevita, Nacusti,*" Tansil replied. "Please sit." He gestured to chairs and a small table that sat close to his desk. "Rest is needed after such a journey."

Zak and Sorwin took seats as Tansil brought water, wine,

and several kinds of tarts, fruits, and salted meats. As the elf moved, Zak took in the rest of this unfamiliar being.

His skin was smooth and dark, matching the wood in his desk. His hair was many hues of brown and gold. The top of his hair was pulled back while the bottom fell loose, reaching just below his shoulders. Zak guessed this was to keep it out of his face as he leaned over the many papers scattered on his desk. His green and gold shirt had a high collar that hugged his neck, accentuating the long lines of his small frame.

Tansil finally set the last plate down, crowded with grapes and three different cheeses Zak didn't recognize, and sat in the third seat at the small table. During all his movements, Tansil didn't make a sound.

"What knowledge have you imparted upon him, Sorwin?"

"Very little, Archmagus. We began his magical studies while fleeing the Consortium and provided the basics of his history. I thought it best that you explain everything in greater detail."

Tansil fixed his eyes on Zak. His look was severe, very focused, but somehow kind as well. Even though Zak had just met the elf, he sensed a heaviness about him, something weighing him down.

"From the beginning, then. Do you know why you were brought here, Zakolor?"

Zak nodded. "I'm the *Nacusti*, and I'm needed to stop Zandorn and the Consortium."

"Yes," Tansil said. "But do you know how you'll do that?"

"Not exactly." Heat flooded his cheeks. He felt like a child in Tansil's presence, a silly child who didn't know who he was or what he was doing. "I know it has something to do with my birth parents, or my magic."

"Yes. It concerns both, actually. You descend from the Belcour bloodline. What do you know of the Guardian War?"

Zak shrugged. "Only what I learned in school. The gods abused their power over the earthly races, so the Guardians helped fight them and force them to sign The Contract."

"Correct, but do you know *how* they helped us, exactly?"

Zak worked to recall his lessons, silently cursing himself for every occasion he daydreamed instead of paying attention. Knowledge was always Kal's strength. A longing for his friend curled painfully through him.

"I think it was something called the Blood Gift," he finally said.

"Right again." Tansil nodded. "Magic is in every living thing, but accessing it is a feat all its own. Elves discovered the secrets of magic and we shared our knowledge with mankind. Thenceforth our races were forever intertwined. The gods created the Guardians to guide us and ensure their will upon the physical plane.

"The Guardians came to us in all shapes and sizes. A hawk and eagle were chosen to protect the skies, bears the mountains, horses the plains, and stags the forests. Two dragons and two phoenixes were also chosen. Since men were born of fire, dragons were appointed Guardians to them. The phoenix, representing longevity and regeneration, was given to elfkind."

"But what exactly is the Blood Gift?" Zak asked.

"It is a sacrifice," Tansil replied. His posture was relaxed but his stare was intense, further accentuated by his glowing eyes. "One of the dragon Guardians sacrificed themselves to give your ancestor—Adrastus Belcour—their power. The Guardians were incredibly powerful, nearly godlike in their own right. That effectively made Adrastus—"

"A god?" Zak was shocked at the words he was hearing.

"Nearly. More like a powerful demigod, at least at first. Over time it became impossible to measure his power as none dared oppose him and he didn't often use magic openly after the war."

"So that would make me..." Zak trailed off, putting the pieces together.

"Also a powerful demigod, like Adrastus."

Tansil's words hung in the air before settling heavily on Zak. It wasn't long ago he thought he had no magic and was wishing for adventure. He couldn't help but wonder if this was all purely chance or if fate had a cruel sense of humor. He shook the thought from his head. He couldn't get distracted now.

"And why is Zandorn after me, or my power, specifically?"

Tansil's eyes narrowed and he shifted in his seat. It was the smallest of movements, but Zak noticed the mention of Zandorn caused a reaction in the elf.

"Zandorn wants to create life. He's experimented with necromancy and various magics, but none have succeeded. Divine magic, or magic of the gods, is one of the only known magics to successfully create life. The Guardians were created by the gods and had similar magic, but they disappeared centuries ago. Many believe they are dead. You are the last known *Nacusti*, meaning you are host to the last known source of divine magic in Valecium."

Zak rocked back in his chair, overwhelmed. His brow furrowed and he felt a headache forming in the back of his skull. He was getting answers to his questions like he wanted. He knew the answers wouldn't be good, but he didn't realize the answers would be so terrifying.

He was afraid to ask any more questions, but he knew he had to understand as much as possible if he hoped to save Kal. "Zandorn needs my power to create life, but why? What is he trying to create?"

"It's not what, but whom. Reviving, to be precise," Sorwin said. He grabbed a vine of grapes and began popping them into his mouth one at a time.

Tansil nodded and continued. "Zandorn was once one of the most talented mages in the Elemental House. He excelled in research and was considered to be a genius. His path changed, though, when his wife bore their child. It was a difficult pregnancy, she was sick and forced to bed rest for most of her carrying months. After the birth of his daughter, Renna, his wife never quite recovered and she remained in bed for several years. Zandorn worked furiously to cure her mysterious ailment, but she died when Renna was still an infant."

"That's terrible," Zak said, looking down at the table. "I didn't know he had a daughter."

"His wife's death was impossible for Zandorn to handle.

It was the first time he felt the sting of inadequacy. In his eyes, he failed to find the answers he needed to heal her. Instead of becoming a broken man, he became doubly focused, and his research turned dark. He began investigating necromancy, soul-binding, and reanimation. Anything that would allow him to raise the dead."

"And you stopped him," Zak said flatly, trying to recall his lessons. "I think I remember learning you arrested him?" His voice went up at the end of his sentence, forming a question.

"Nearly." Tansil's face darkened despite his bright eyes. "I didn't want to. He was a close friend and was grieving, but the practices he pursued were dangerous to the world."

"We saw on our way here," Sorwin said. "The Rot has reached as far south as Lindomer."

Tansil's jaw muscles visibly tightened. It was a few moments before he spoke again. "Magic is in all things, Zakolor. It has a flow akin to a river."

As the elf spoke, the water in one of the pitchers on the table gently floated into the air, forming a circle. It began rotating—flowing—like a small river.

Zak's eyes widened. Neither Sorwin nor Tansil had moved. Who was doing this? How were they doing it?

Tansil continued. "Necromancy, or any unnatural practice, is a disruption to that flow." The elf's eyes briefly flicked to Sorwin, giving him the slightest of nods.

Sorwin lobbed one of his grapes at the miniature river. As it passed through, it formed a small hole in the water.

"Some isolated practices, while still harmful, can be repaired," Tansil said. The small stream condensed slightly to fill the hole from the grape. "However, extended perversions of magic create unprecedented levels of decay."

Sorwin picked up a knife from the table and held it in the small, floating river. As the water flowed and hit the knife, the stream parted. The second stream wove wildly, trying to reconnect with the rest of the river. Before it could, it began to evaporate, disappearing before Zak's eyes. The rest of the small river flowed through the air, settling carefully back into the pitcher.

"Do you see why we must stop Zandorn now, Zakolor? He is killing Valecium, killing magic itself. That is what the Rot is showing us."

Zak nodded. This was way more information than he was expecting. After so much time without answers, processing everything Tansil had shared was difficult. Zak had something of his own to share too.

"My friend Kalbick was kidnapped," he said abruptly. "I'll do whatever you want to stop Zandorn as long as we rescue him." His resolve hardened as he spoke about Kal. In Zak's increasingly complicated world, his determination to save his friend was something he never questioned.

"Yes, Sorwin informed me of the situation. We will do everything we can to save him." Tansil paused for a few moments, searching for the right words. "I think you should prepare for several outcomes, Zakolor. We might save Kalbick, and we might not. Unfortunately, many lives have been lost in the war with the Consortium."

As Tansil spoke, Zak shook his head. "No, there is only

one outcome: we will save Kal." He raised his voice and felt a sudden heat course through his body, concentrating in his hands as he gripped the arms of his chair.

What was that? Zak looked down, and for the briefest moment, he could have sworn his skin was green.

When he looked up again, Sorwin and Tansil were staring at him. Sorwin's expression looked curious and concerned, while Tansil's eyes widened in what he assumed was surprise.

"I'm sorry," Zak apologized. "I don't know what came over me."

"Zakolor, did you just—" Tansil started.

He was interrupted as the door to the chambers opened. Zak immediately recognized Olivia as she entered the room.

"Archmagus Tansil," she said, bowing her head momentarily. "Sorry for the interruption. I was sent to inform you and High Magus Sorwin that an emergency council meeting has been called. I'm to escort you there now."

Sorwin inhaled and exhaled deeply. Tansil continued to study Zak for a few moments longer before responding.

"Very well," Tansil said, standing and crossing the room with fluid grace. Let's not keep them waiting." He turned to look back at Zak. You should come as well, *Nacusti*," he said before continuing out of the room without a sound.

Zak grimaced at the use of his title but nodded and followed Sorwin to the door. He knew what a council meeting was, the elders used to have them in Densba all the time. He had no idea how council meetings worked with the League of Kingdoms though. Who would be there? And why had Tansil asked him to come?

Olivia stood by the door waiting for Sorwin and Zak to file out.

"Hi," Zak said, stopping in front of Olivia. "I'm Za-kolor."

"No," Olivia said.

Zak's face scrunched in confusion. "No, what?"

"No talking," she responded, pushing him into the hall-way and closing the door behind them.

CHAPTER 14

THE TEST

Kal woke slowly. His head pounded in rebellion to his consciousness as he squinted against the daylight. He was back in the large, open room Renna first brought him to. He tried to wipe his eyes, but when his hands refused to move he looked up and saw them chained to the rough rock wall above his head. His third escape attempt of the week was unsuccessful, so he was not at all surprised to find his new accommodations.

The door to his right opened and Renna walked into the room with a brisk gait. Even though he had only known her for a few weeks, he could tell she was irritated. She was not one to show her emotions often.

"Good, you're awake," she said, stopping a few feet in front of him. "What have you learned this time?"

"Not to run away during exercise hours," he answered reluctantly.

"And why not?" she questioned further.

"Because I'll get knocked out by a gods-cursed nox demon."

"Exactly. Oh, Kalbick. You really have disappointed me so far. You have a rare gift, an incredible amount of potential, yet you insist on resisting me and my best efforts to educate you, to make you strong. Don't you want to be strong?"

"I will be, someday. I'll escape here or be rescued, and I'll join the League and get trained. Then I'll come back and wreck this cursed place!" he threatened, rattling his chains.

He knew it carried little weight based on her laughter. She took a few steps closer and crouched before him, running her hand through his hair and down the side of his cheek. He tried to jerk away but had nowhere to go.

"Now, now, no need to get all worked up. If we redirect that energy, you can be trained right here, with me. If you follow me, you could summon a 'gods-cursed nox demon' yourself. How does that sound?"

"What do you want with me? Why am I here?" he asked. She never gave him straight answers, only ever harped on his potential. "I know Burvenin was supposed to kidnap Zakolor instead of me, I overheard him talking to Zandorn. Why bother keeping me? And what did you want with Zak?"

Renna paused, seeming to ponder his questions. "It's true, you were kidnapped by accident. But you proved yourself in the Test, and I think you could become something great."

"A test? I passed a test, so you're keeping me prisoner?"

"*The* Test, Kalbick," she stated, standing up and walking around the room. She picked at some fruit as she passed by the table which was laden with another spread of enticing delicacies.

"The cages you were in when you first arrived here. That was the Test. You fought to survive. My father's followers are small in number. We need every able body we can get our hands on, but they have to *want* to live, to survive. That's why we take those showing their determination. We can't afford to waste soldiers like the League."

"You're wrong! The League does no such thing!" he countered.

"Oh no? Why do you think they recruit so young? They can't wait to throw as many soldiers and mages at us as possible. Have you any idea how uneven the fatalities to each side have been over the last century? They can't even find us! They hope to flood us out with sheer numbers, thinking someone will stumble across us at some point. We choose to strike when we want and where we want. This is not a war, not yet. It is merely a sad attempt at a resistance."

Kal was furious and confused by her words. He tried to shake them off, focusing on gaining more useful information. The more he knew, the more helpful he could be when he finally escaped and joined the League. "That explains why you want me, but not Zakolor," he redirected.

"Zakolor has something my father needs to complete his research."

"What is it?"

"A power he doesn't understand. He holds it within while others could benefit from its use. Much like you are doing with your gift," she said.

Kal felt a pressure in his head. He recognized it as Renna trying to sway the direction of his thoughts with her Influence.

"My gift?" Kal grunted. He felt he was getting distracted, but he couldn't remember what from.

"Yes, are you not aware?" Renna asked. "You have some magical prowess so I assumed your magus had informed you. Usually a mage's magic rejects foreign magic. It is a natural instinct to protect the host from curses or possession. Your magic is quite unique. It reaches for and desires contact with other energies. It has an absorbent quality I have never seen before. All I need do is feed you, just a little," she trailed off, approaching him again.

"Feed me? What in the Three Fires are you talking about?" he asked, getting more and more nervous.

"Don't worry, it shouldn't hurt much," the corner of Renna's mouth twitched as she said the last part, fighting a smile. She crouched down and held her hand over his head, allowing her magic to flow out to meet his.

As expected, his magic reached out of its own volition and latched onto hers. It began absorbing her power, slowly at first, and then building as it became nourished.

Kal's eyes closed and his head tipped back.

Renna knew he was in a trance of sorts. "You could be amazing, under my tutelage. Don't you want to be amazing, Kalbick?"

"I could...be amazing?" His voice was different, much more monotone.

"You already are," she answered, allowing herself to smile.

CHAPTER 15

THE COUNCIL

Zak plunked down the stairs, his legs still heavy from the days of riding to Tor'alan. Ahead, Tansil glided down the steps—silent and swift—to the main hall of the Center. Sorwin and Olivia followed quickly behind.

Euphemius was waiting by an open door, shifting his weight front and back with apparent impatience. His expression was sharp and unmoving.

"Come," was all he said as he turned and stomped through the open door.

As Zak followed the rest of the group, he couldn't help but wonder if the short merchant's emotional range only extended from angry to perturbed.

Zak was in a large, lavish room. Every inch of the enormous walls were covered with tapestries and paintings depicting the histories of each kingdom in the League. Across from the door was a hollow, octagonal wooden table with such detail Zak thought it must have taken years to carve. Surrounding the table were nearly two dozen finely dressed people Zak didn't recognize. He assumed they must make up the council.

Tansil and Sorwin headed toward the left side of the table while Euphemius and Oliva headed toward the right. Olivia looked back at Zak momentarily. Was that fear in her eyes? He followed Sorwin the opposite direction but kept his eyes on Olivia as she turned away.

Everyone moved toward the table, standing in front of precisely placed chairs. Zak noticed that at each point of the octagonal table was an ornately carved wooden armchair flanked by two smaller, simpler chairs. Tansil stood in front of one of the chairs at a point. Sorwin instructed Zak to take the chair to the Archmagus' left as he stood by the one on the right.

"The council of the League of Kingdoms is now in session. Please be seated," said a young attendant off to Zak's left. The room echoed with rustling fabric and chairs sliding on the stone floor as almost two dozen council members took their seats.

Once everyone was seated, official names and titles were declared to establish attendance for the records. As Archmagus and High Magus, Tansil and Sorwin represented the house of elemental magic. The Archlumen and Archalium were accounted for, along with the leaders of four countries in the League (Sorwin spoke again, as he also represented Darlangson). Each leader sat at one of the octagonal points, flanked by two attendants. Several Center officials, military generals, and merchants were also present, seated in the spaces between the leaders.

After each title and name was announced Zak felt more

and more nauseous. What was he doing in this room of pow-erful people who controlled the League? Yes, he knew he wanted to join the League. Yes, he now knew he inherited a lot of power from his bloodline. He didn't think he was ready to be in *this* room though. A voice pulled him out of his spinning thoughts.

"Welcome, everyone. Thank you for coming on such short notice," said a young man at one of the points of the table. He spoke with a shaky voice and a practiced tone, as though he had rehearsed his words several times.

"As you all know," continued the young man, "my grandfather created this council decades ago to keep peace between our proud nations as we battle a common enemy. To do so, he also created the role of High King to keep order among us."

A tall, lean man with a hooked nose standing behind the young man bent down and whispered in his ear. The tall man's face was as long and thin as his body and further accentuated by a severely pointed chin. He appeared to have a permanent scowl etched into his unimpressible face.

The young man nodded and blushed. "Yes, well, I sup-pose I can skip the history and move to the reason we are all here," he said. "As your High King, Marius Fern, I called this meeting to discuss the arrival of the *Nacusti* in Tor'alan."

The council erupted in surprise and questions. It was hard to understand anyone, but one voice cut above the noise.

"More secrets, Tansil?" shouted a plump man with fierce eyes and a brown beard. "Why weren't we told of the *Nacusti's* existence?" The room quieted, waiting for a response from the elf.

"For his safety and yours, Archalium Vermig." Tansil answered in the same cool tone he had used with Zak in his office. "The less people who knew of his existence, the better. We couldn't risk the information finding its way to the Consortium."

The room erupted in fervor again. Zak gathered that most of the people in the room weren't aware of his existence before now, let alone his travels to Tor'alan. He could feel himself shrinking in his chair as more than a few looks were directed at him and questions lobbed his way. He resisted the urge and lifted his chin slightly, remembering lessons his mother gave him on proper table etiquette. He wasn't sure if dinner posture translated to League council meetings, but he thought it couldn't hurt.

Marius whacked a small gavel on the table, attempting to bring order to the chaos. The room eventually quieted, but the silence only fueled the increasing tension.

"Everyone will be filled in on the details in time, I promise," Marius said. "In the meantime, we need a plan. I received a few reports of the *Nacusti's* travels. It seems the Consortium is aware he is the *Nacusti* and that he is here in Tor'alan. Tansil, you know Zandorn best. Do you believe he will organize an attack on Tor'alan? Will he come after the *Nacusti*?"

Zandorn...coming after me? Zak's stomach lurched.

"I don't believe so, Your Majesty," Tansil said.

"You don't believe, but you can't be sure?" Vermig scoffed. "And you wish us to stake our future on this belief?"

"We have gained little ground since Zandorn's defection, but neither has he. Currently, we are unable to locate his exact whereabouts, though we know he resides somewhere in the Wastelands. All I ask is a few years of bided time until we can further explore Zakolor's power. He is our best hope in finding and defeating Zandorn," Tansil explained.

"A few years is a long time to remain idle, Archmagus," Euphemius said. "Idle is expensive."

"We will not be idle, Mr. Van Illia, we will be refocused," Tansil replied.

"I still think a ceasefire could be negotiated," Vermig said. "He has been equally unsuccessful in the war during the last century. Perhaps Zandorn would consider peace or reabsorption by the League."

"Hah! That is hardly conceivable, Archalium," mocked a woman to Zak's right. He recalled her name and title from earlier: Jeppida Qor, Prime Minister of the Republic of Evartia. She stuck out in his memory as the only leader who wasn't a noble. "He has proven time and again he will pursue his goals to the end. Not to mention the people of the League, or at least Evartia, refuse to consider reabsorption. If you crave the secrets of his research, why not put in a formal request with the Consortium?"

Vermig shot a dirty look at Jeppida. "How dare you—"

"What do you mean by refocused, Tansil?" A woman dressed in brilliant lilac silks interrupted the budding argument.

Zak couldn't remember her name, but he appreciated her tactful intervention.

"Thank you, Archlumen Sashina," Tansil said. "Instead of searching for Zandorn, we will search for what he wants. We know he wants Zakolor, the *Nacusti*."

He gestured to Zak, and dozens of eyes landed on him. He flinched every time someone said *Nacusti*.

Tansil continued. "And luckily we have him. I know Zandorn will not attempt an assault on Tor'alan. The results would be too uncertain for his sacrifice. The only thing he wants as much as the Blood Gift is a Druid."

"You wish to change our strategy now, elf?" asked a man in full armor. Again his name escaped Zak, but he knew he was a general. Debate broke out after his question, voices were raised and insults began to fly. Marius used his gavel again to call order back to the room.

"What are you proposing?" Marius asked Tansil. The king's brow was sweating and Zak empathized with his apparent anxiety. This was all moving too fast for him to follow.

"That we find the Druids first," Tansil said flatly. "Until now they have hidden themselves adequately, but they are running out of time. The Rot is spreading across our kingdoms and destroying magic with it, limiting their options and abilities to hide. With the resurfacing of the *Nacusti* this century-long stalemate will now accelerate. Zandorn will stop toying with our forces and begin to make decisive and purposeful moves. He won't come to Tor'alan directly, not at first, but we need to be prepared to anticipate and defeat those moves." He had to shout the last part as more protests broke out. Marius used his gavel a third time to quiet the council. Tension covered the king's face.

"It's a waste of time," Vermig said. "The Druids have been in hiding for more than a century. They predicted the unnatural arts that Zandorn pursued, what makes you think they won't see you coming?"

"They were unified back then, they had a clarity that is unattainable today," Tansil explained. "They split up and hid themselves in their forests. They aren't as strong on their own. Last week I received a report of a Druid sighting not two days' ride from here, near the Wastelands. We need to find them before Zandorn does. If he gets ahold of them and corrupts their magic it would be disastrous. They are so closely tied to the fabric of nature it could end our world entirely."

Zak felt his eyes widen and mouth drop open. It was one thing to hear about the end of the world, or to see the Rot spreading. It was completely different to hear Tansil explain an exact scenario of *how* the world could end.

The tall man leaned down and whispered into Marius' ear again. "How do you plan to find the Druids, Archmagus?" Marius asked.

"With Sorwin's assistance, we have crafted an effective strategy."

The man in the armor spoke again. "Why do we not flood the forests and Wastelands with our armies? The Druids will have no hole to hide in."

"You know why, General Lupa," Euphemius said, addressing the man in armor. "The last time we did so we lost a third of our forces. The Wastelands are uninhabitable, they drain the life out of any living thing that enters. Only Zandorn knows how to live there."

"What is your plan, Archmagus?" Sashina asked.

"We will use an *indagomius*. *Nacusti* magic is similar to Druid magic—a cousin of sorts. If Zakolor uses the device, it should lead us to the nearest Druid."

Zak had no idea what an *indagomius* was, but now he knew he would be needed to help find the Druids. A few whispers passed between attendants and leaders, but no one spoke out against Tansil's idea.

"Very well, Archmagus. Please begin as soon as possible," Marius said.

"Of course, Your Majesty," Tansil said, bowing his head.

After a few other minor updates, Marius adjourned the meeting. As everyone stood to leave, Zak was lost in a haze. The gravity of his situation became clearer by the second. Even a mage as powerful as Tansil, an elf more than half a millennia old (according to Sorwin) and the leader of the League's elemental forces, was resting his hope on Zak's young shoulders. It made him question—and even fear—the unknown power inside him.

"Let's get you some rest, you've earned it," Sorwin said, coming up behind Zak and gently patting his shoulder.

"Yes, that would help," Zak muttered, still lost in thought. He stood and followed Sorwin toward the door. He felt dozens of eyes trained on him, the curiosity of the council somehow shrinking the giant room while extending the walk to the exit. Only one person moved toward him.

"Sorwin, I was wondering if I might have a word." It was the tall man that kept whispering to Marius during the meeting. IIis voice was unnaturally prickly and made Zak uncomfortable.

For the first time since meeting Sorwin, Zak thought he saw the mage look reluctant to speak with someone.

"Yes, Limba Dar? What was it you required?" Sorwin asked with a sigh.

"Actually, I was hoping to speak with the *Nacusti*. It's Zakolor, isn't it?" The tall, thin man fixed his abnormally large eyes on Zak. He attempted what may have been a sincere smile but his face twisted into something darker.

"Yes, nice to meet you," Zak said, minding his manners. Why did this man make him nervous?

"The High King Marius holds you in great esteem, young mage. As do I. We look forward to your...tenure here in Tor'alan."

"Thank you, sir. I owe everything to Sorwin. He saved my life, several times."

"Yes, yes, I've heard your rather exciting story. I was curious, would you consider—"

"No, he will not," Sorwin interrupted loudly and sternly.

Limba Dar's words caught in his throat. He looked surprised to be interrupted. He sneered at Sorwin but kept his words sweet. "My dear Magerus, you do not know what it is I was going to ask the boy."

"Yes, I do. He's not interested. Now, I need to get my apprentice to dinner and bed before he falls over from exhaustion. Goodnight, Limba Dar." Sorwin tilted his head in a bow a fraction of an inch and steered Zak out of the council chambers, down the hallway, and toward the front doors of the large castle.

"What did he want to ask me?" Zak asked when they were a good distance away from the castle.

"He wanted you to be the High King's trophy, and his by proxy."

"What?"

"They would create a position for you, something that rings with reverence but in reality would be meaningless. You are something of a decoration to Limba Dar. He is a greed-driven man who collects all the power and money he can sink his claws into. He slithered his way to Marius' shoulder to whisper twisted words to his advantage. Because of him, and Euphemius, and several others like them, the League isn't what it once was. It is divided, Zakolor. That is one of the many reasons why we need you. You will be the standard we unite behind."

"How?" Zak stopped in his tracks. All the pressure of his new power and the expectations upon him kept piling, growing, mounting. He hadn't been in Tor'alan half a day yet and already he felt like he was drowning.

"How?" Sorwin parroted, facing Zak.

"Yes, how? How do I unite a divided League? If people like you and Tansil can't do it, what could I do that would be any different?"

Zak saw concern in Sorwin's expression. The mage paused before responding.

"I know this isn't fair, that it's far more than you ever must have imagined." Sorwin closed the few feet between them and rested his hand on Zak's shoulder. "You won't be alone. Tansil and I will be guiding you the whole time, I promise."

Zak nodded. He believed Sorwin, or believed he would try to keep his promise. But that wasn't an answer, and he wasn't sure he could live up to their expectations.

"Come on, let's get you fed and to sleep. We'll start explaining the plan to you tomorrow," Sorwin said.

CHAPTER 16

INDAGOMIUS

After a fitful night of sleep—if he could call it that, given all the tossing and turning—Zak woke early to find fresh clothes set out for him. He had spent the night in an extra room in the Dormitory, a rigidly symmetrical building that served as housing for junior students of the mage academy. He stretched, working the soreness from his road-weary muscles as he quickly changed and left his room. Zak wandered his way to the mess hall, silently thanking Sorwin for giving him a brief tour last evening.

Mages and apprentices alike milled about and sat at the various wooden tables, eating breakfast and quietly whispering, shooting glances his way when it seemed he wasn't looking. As Zak moved through the breakfast line, he felt his face flush, realizing they were probably talking about him and his sudden appearance.

Feeling even more alone than ever in a room full of people, he picked up a plate and quickly piled the nearest food on, not even looking at what he grabbed. He kept his head down and moved to a table in the corner, putting his back to the stone wall and trying to ignore the rest of the diners.

"You must be Zakolor," said a voice.

Zak looked up to see a tall man with jet-black braids pulled back and fastened with a leather strap and silver clasp. He looked a few years older than Zak, but his sharp features and confident stature made it difficult to tell.

The man held out a hand toward Zak. "Bazil Ben," he said with a stoic yet kind face.

Zak hesitated for a moment before offering his hand in return. He couldn't afford to be rude to the only person in a room full of people who spoke to him.

"Well-met," he responded. "How did you know my name?"

Bazil put down his plate and took the seat across from Zak, digging into his eggs and various breakfast meats.

"Word travels fast around here, as I'm sure you noticed." He motioned with his thumb over his shoulder to the students and staff still stealing not-so-subtle glances at Zak.

"Do you know what they're saying?" Zak asked, feeling his face turn hot again at the question. He felt odd asking for information about himself but thought it was better to know.

Bazil blinked at Zak, holding his fork in midair. "Mostly 'why was a boy from the southern isles escorted personally by Sorwin Darlangson and whisked into a Council meeting on his first day in Tor'alan?' Rumors sprang to life within an hour of your arrival. Everything from 'He's a spy!' to prophecies and conspiracies, naturally."

If only they knew I have just as many questions about my situation as they do, Zak thought.

"Um, sorry, and who are you, Bazil?" He flushed again, feeling awkward for sounding skeptical. He wished Kal was here. His friend would know exactly what to do and how to do it gracefully.

Bazil's expression remained stoic. "A fair question. I'm a priest in the League. I teach a few classes here at the academy when I'm not in the field. Sorwin sent me, he thought you might need a friendly face to keep an eye on you while he's occupied."

Zak silently wondered what Sorwin's definition of 'friendly face' was as Bazil's was mostly blank. But he was certainly grateful for the company.

"He mentioned yesterday he'd be...explaining things to me?" Zak's inflection went up at the end of his statement, unsure how much the priest knew.

Bazil nodded. "I'm to take you to him when you're done eating."

Without a moment's hesitation, Zak slid his untouched plate of food to the middle of the table. "I'm done," he said. He couldn't bear another minute in this room with the constant glances and whispers.

Bazil shrugged. "Suit yourself." He shoveled in a few more bites before grabbing their plates and motioning for Zak to follow him.

Zak was thankful Bazil moved at a quick pace, emerging from the large double doors of the mess hall and crossing the grounds to the Center's castle. They scaled the winding staircase to Tansil's office.

Bazil knocked on the door. After a brief pause it opened,

revealing Olivia. She said nothing as she stepped aside, allowing the pair to enter.

What is she doing here? Zak wondered.

They walked into the office and saw Tansil and Sorwin standing over a small device on the Archmagus' desk, talking quietly.

"Ah, welcome! Thank you, Bazil, for bringing Zakolor," Sorwin said in greeting.

Bazil tipped his head and closed the door, standing at attention near the door by Olivia.

"How are you, Zakolor?" Tansil asked.

"I'm fine," he lied. With little sleep and a mountain of anxiety-driven questions, he was now regretting not eating breakfast.

Tansil's eyes narrowed but he said nothing. Zak felt transparent, as though the elf could see directly into his mind.

"Splendid," Sorwin said, moving the conversation along. "We only require a few moments of your time. Now, this is a wonderful little device called an *indagomius*."

He picked up the palm-sized purple diamond from Tansil's desk and held it out for Zak to inspect. It was cut in a pentagon shape and set in gold brackets.

"Without getting too detailed, it tracks and detects specific magical signatures. All it requires is a sample of the magic it is tracking."

"So this is how we'll find the Druid?" Zak queried.

"Precisely," Sorwin replied.

"You have a sample of the Druid's magic?"

"Of course not, how would we get that?"

"I'm confused."

Tansil chimed in. "Druid and Guardian magic have very similar signatures. We are hoping that by sampling your *Nacusti* magic we can pinpoint the Druid's location from the recent sighting. It may prove tedious at first, we'll need the Druid to use a significant level of magic all at once or build up use in one area for the *indagomius* to track it. This will be tricky since they are actively hiding and avoiding just that."

"I see," Zak said, appreciating Tansil's direct explanation. Zak had grown very fond of Sorwin but the man could be entirely baffling at times. "What do you need me to do?"

"We need you to hit this jewel with everything you've got," Sorwin said, placing the *indagomius* on the floor in the middle of the room and backing away. "It absorbs any magic it comes in contact with. I believe simple flames will work. Make sure to put everything into it, though. The bigger the sample the more easily it will track the Druid. Whenever you're ready." He clasped his hands in front of him.

Zak glanced around the room at Tansil, Sorwin, Bazil, and Olivia. He felt nervous with the audience, his stomach clenching.

This is it, he thought. *I'm finally getting one step closer to you, Kal.*

His resolve to find Kal gave him strength as he moved back, positioning himself a few paces from the *indagomius*. He closed his eyes and took a moment to center himself, finding his magic and feeling its power. He opened his eyes and raised his hands, directing his palms toward the *indagomius*.

"*Ignis*," he whispered.

Emerald fire streaked from his hands through the air towards the jewel. The *indagomius* bounced and shook violently on the floor as it absorbed the fire. The streams of flame lit everything in the room with a green hue. Zak scrunched his face, feeling the heat of his flames.

"See if you can give it more, Zak!" Sorwin shouted over the roaring fire as it tore through the air.

Zak reached for his magic again, pulling more toward his hands and doubled his efforts. The fire grew bigger and louder, filling more space between him and the jewel. It felt like he was channeling the spell for an eternity, though it was probably less than a minute. He released the magic, dropping his hands as the last of the flames disappeared inside the jewel.

Tansil strode forward to check the *indagomius*. He picked it up, turning it over a few times.

Zak leaned forward, resting his hands on his knees as a few beads of sweat rolled down his face, breathing hard from the exertion.

"We'll need a bit more, if you're able," Tansil said.

Zak looked up and could tell from the elf's expression he felt sorry making the request.

Sorwin came forward, dabbing Zak's forehead and checking his student over.

"I'm fine," Zak assured his magus. He nodded toward Tansil. "I'll do it again."

Tansil reciprocated the nod and replaced the *indagomius* to its spot on the floor.

Zak repeated his process, steadying his breath and finding his magic. Again he pulled on his magic, but this time he pulled on everything he could. He held back before, afraid to test his limits after what he'd learned from Sorwin and Tansil. If he really was the powerful demigod-like mage that they claimed him to be, he didn't want to hurt anyone in the room. But now, with a chance to find Kal, his determination outweighed his fear.

"*Ignis,*" he said again, this time louder. Immediately the emerald flames erupted from his hands with more than double the force and speed as before. He couldn't see the *indagomius* through the fiery maelstrom but he could feel its presence, could feel it absorbing his magic.

More, he heard a voice whisper. It was deep and rumbling. *You can do more.*

Where was that coming from? He puzzled for a moment, briefly looking at his companion's faces. No one else seemed to hear it.

In the midst of his confusion he realized the voice was right, he could do more. He could *feel* that he could do more, that he had a vast well of untapped magic inside him. He reached for it now, pulling it forward and streaming it into his spell.

That's it, the voice rumbled. *Now you're starting to see.*

The flames grew even larger, whipping up a wind that knocked over books and candles on Tansil's desk and pulled loose papers into the flame. They burned so fast and so hot there wasn't even ash left behind.

He could barely see Tansil or Sorwin anymore. He saw their arms waving and mouths moving but the torrent of flame drowned out any other sound.

Brief thoughts tugged at his attention. Should he stop? Is this safe? Is it enough to find the Druid?

You're almost there, said the voice. *Keep going.*

Zak wondered why he was listening to the voice, but he could feel it was right. The *indagomius* felt almost at capacity. He refocused on the jewel, pushing his magic even harder.

A flicker of movement caught his eye. Something was on his hand—no, not on it, but *changing* it. From the ends of his fingertips, a wave crawled up to his wrists, turning his skin green in its wake. It continued up his arms, and his eyes widened in shock as green scales grew on his skin. Dark black claws sprouted from his fingertips as he screamed in confusion and fear.

Zak fell backward and the spell broke as the last of the flames disappeared. He quickly sat back up, looking down at his hands.

He hadn't imagined it, they were covered in emerald scales and the black claws clicked together as he opened and closed his palms.

Sorwin rushed forward and kneeled in front of Zak, stopping just short of touching him. His face scrunched in concern and surprise.

Zak's eyes were wide and his mouth hung open, feeling so overwhelmed he couldn't form words.

"What?" was all Zak could manage. He looked between Sorwin and his arms, utterly confused and terrified.

"Everything's going to be fine, Zak," Sorwin said. His voice sounded more calm than his face looked. "Bazil, here please."

The priest sprung forward, his stoic expression lifted with surprise. That made Zak feel even more worried.

Bazil's hands glowed with a soft turquoise light as they hovered over Zak's arms. "It's not foreign magic," he announced. "It's his magic that did this."

Sorwin, still crouched in front of Zak, turned to look at Tansil behind him. The elf had picked up the *indagomius* and was watching Bazil work.

"It's an effect of the Guardian magic," Tansil said. "Without control, the power can overwhelm a *Nacusti*."

"Can we fix it?" Zak asked, trying not to move his arms as Bazil continued his inspection.

"In time you'll be able to do so yourself, but until then we'll have to treat it as best we can."

Bazil nodded. "It's complex but with a mixture of salves and potions you should be back to normal in a few days. Though..." he hesitated. "The shedding process will be uncomfortable."

"Shedding?" Zak shrieked.

"Yes, well, the scales are going to fall off," Bazil answered, back to his normally stoic self.

"I..." Zak stumbled over his words. "I heard a voice." He turned to Tansil, who seemed to have the most answers. Zak wondered how odd that was for a mage.

Tansil was silent for a few moments. "That is unique. A few *Nacusti* have claimed to be able to commune with their Guardians, though it's impossible for anyone to confirm the claims as only the *Nacusti* can engage their spirit."

"I'll need him brought to the healing wards," Bazil said.

He stood and dug through a satchel at his side, pulling out a roll of linen bandages. "Best to wrap you up unless you want new rumors flying around that you're a demon."

Zak's stomach twisted as he absorbed Tansil's information and Bazil's accurate logic.

"Who's to say they'd just be rumors?" he joked, though no one—including himself—cracked a smile. He nodded his agreement as Bazil began wrapping his arms in the bandages. "Did it work, at least?" he asked Tansil, glancing at the *indagomius*.

"It seems we have enough for now, though more of your magic will only improve our efforts." He crossed the office to a table made entirely of glass. It had a map of all Valecium etched into the top—the four nations of the League, the southern isles, the elven and dwarven territories, and even the Wastelands. As he carefully set the *indagomious* onto a small pedestal in the center of the table, it glowed dimly and hummed, filling the air with a soft vibration.

"What happens now?" Zak asked.

"Now, we wait," Tansil answered.

CHAPTER 17

TIMING IS EVERYTHING

Renna sat at the enormous table in her formal chambers overlooking a gorge with vegetation below.

"My father really performed a miracle getting these plants to grow," she told Gunther.

The large man lumbered around the table, placing various dishes laden with fruits and meats. He picked up a golden pitcher and refilled Renna's goblet with pemberry wine in a surprisingly graceful motion.

Since Gunther never spoke—and Renna loved that about him—she continued. "The Wastelands were uninhabitable before my father arrived, you know. He's the only one to successfully survive here in centuries. He risked everything for me, for us, for our family..." She drifted off, an almost sad lilt in her voice.

Her musings were interrupted by the door swinging open and rebounding off the wall with a bang. Burvenin stormed across the room with Karazul trailing casually behind.

"You could have *killed* me, you sewer rat!" Burvenin yelled, stomping to the table and angrily ripping a drumstick off the nearest plate with baked poultry.

Karazul sauntered in and sat smoothly and quietly, as silent as a shadow. "One misdirected fireball, that's all it was." He winked at Renna.

She wasn't impressed by his charm; he was one of the few people that unnerved Renna. She found him more annoying than anything, though.

"Keep your hands off my magic," Burvenin shot back through a mouthful of meat. "Deflect your own fireballs if you want. Oh wait, that's right, you can't! You couldn't start a fire without us enchanting totems for you." He took another giant bite of his drumstick, squirting grease everywhere.

Repulsive, Renna thought.

"You're right, I can't use magic. But neither can you when I get close enough." A dangerous smile found Karazul's lips as he played with a dagger.

Burvenin's smug expression waned as he watched the knife dancing in the assassin's hands.

"Is that fear I see, Burvenin?" Renna piped in. "You may be smarter than I thought."

Burvenin scowled and opened his mouth—presumably to retort—but the door opened with a loud bang again, cutting him off.

Zandorn swept across the room toward the table. He was followed closely by a pale woman Renna didn't recognize. She was dressed in fine grey and gold silks that draped and knotted, flowing like a fabric waterfall as she walked.

Nobility, Renna judged based on the woman's gait and attire. What really caught Renna's attention was the large diamond on the woman's necklace, not because of the stone, but rather what was trapped inside. Renna felt the pulse of powerful magic within the precious stone.

Zandorn and the woman took seats at the table. "Good, now that we're all here, we can begin," Zandorn said. "Let's finish this quickly. I have work that needs my attention more than you lot," he added. "How faired the raid?"

"Well enough, sir," Burvenin said. "We lost but two men while the League lost nearly two dozen. We destroyed the village as well."

"Good. Any recruits?"

"Several fine additions, sir." Burvenin hesitated momentarily, debating his next statement. "Sir, if I may, I'd like to make a formal complaint about—"

"About what?" Zandorn barked. His eyes narrowed as he looked between Burvenin and Karazul. "You two can kill each other after I'm done with you, not before."

"Yes, sir," they answered in unison.

"Now, Renna, dearest Daughter. Save me from their ignorance with good news of Kalbick."

"He is progressing splendidly, Father," she replied. "His power and mastery of the arts grows daily as his objection and insubordination diminish. The more his magic feeds upon mine, the more his mind reshapes its will to follow my own." It was becoming too easy to shame those two buffoons, not that she even cared.

"When will he be field ready?"

"A few months at most."

"Perfect. This will work with our new plan," Zandorn thought out loud.

"New plan, Father?" Renna asked. Her eyes darted to the mystery woman seated at the table.

"Yes. Due to the lackluster kidnap attempts of Burvenin and Karazul, we are without the *Nacusti*. Even worse, the League now has him in their hold. My former magus, Tansil, is too familiar with my tactics, so we will play right into his hand. He knows I wouldn't risk attacking Tor'alan, and he is right. It is too well-fortified at the moment for our forces to penetrate. My only option is to find a Druid," he stated.

"A Druid?" Burvenin queried.

"Yes," Zandorn said. "Their magic is like a cousin to the *Nacusti's*. And their reincarnation abilities are fascinating. I believe a Druid would prove a fine substitute in my experiments."

"But how will we find—" Burvenin started.

"It's simple. Druids govern forests. They hide amongst the trees. You, Burvenin, and you, Karazul, will comb every single forest in Valecium if you have to. You will find a Druid, capture it, and bring it back here. I will view this as repentance for your prior failings."

Renna smiled as both Burvenin and Karazul's faces wrenched in shock. "But...but that'll take years!" Burvenin wailed. "Sir, you can't honestly expect us to—"

"Can't I?!" Zandorn slammed both hands down on the table. "You exhaust my patience, Burvenin. Who took you in when you left Tor'alan in disgrace? Who sustained you with an unnaturally long life? Who continues to house you even after your fruitless missions? You will do this. You will do this because I command it. You need no further reason and need not question it. Are we clear?"

"Yes, my lord," he answered meekly.

"You." Zandorn pointed at Karazul. "Use your gift to expel the magic from any trees you find. Then they cannot hide any place you have been."

"Yes, sir," Karazul said. "That will kill the trees, just to be clear."

Zandorn leveled a withering stare at Karazul. The assassin raised his hands in submission.

"Now, since finding a Druid is of the utmost importance, I am not leaving the task solely in your incapable hands. As fortune would have it, Queen Ymona sought me out just as I needed her help." He gestured to the woman in silks. She nodded, her lilac hair shifting as she acknowledged his introduction.

"Thank you, Zandorn. It is a privilege to be here. Recently, my kingdom, Evartia, rebelled against my brother and me. We were twin monarchs, but he did not make it out of the war entirely whole." Her hand softly touched the diamond at her neck.

So that's *who's in there, her brother*, Renna thought. *How delicious.*

"How does an overthrown queen and gem-sized brother help our cause, Father?" Renna asked, keeping one eye on Ymona. She was happy to see the queen recoil, though she wasn't sure if it was due to disrespect for her status, her brother, or both.

Ymona's cheeks turned a darker shade, getting closer to matching her lilac hair. Renna was impressed as the woman quickly recovered her composure and offered a delightfully fake smile, no doubt perfected from years at court.

"You must be Renna. It is a pleasure to meet the daughter of the esteemed Zandorn. While I am currently without my kingdom, I am not without resources. Many of Evartia's army and navy remain loyal to me and my brother. They are on their way here now."

Renna eyed the woman for a moment before turning to her father. "We're finally going on the offensive, then? No more silly raids?"

Zandorn nodded. "There will still be raids, but we're finally ready to begin this war in earnest. We'll use our forces and Ymona's army to create havoc in the most heavily wooded areas, further eliminating potential hiding places for the Druids."

Renna smiled. "Good, it's about time we showed the League what we're truly capable of." She thought for a moment. "What of the *Nacusti*? Have we no need for him if we capture a Druid?"

"No, not entirely. Even if my experiments are successful with the Druid, I will still need a massive amount of power to revive your mother. I can think of no greater source than the *Nacusti*."

"Then we bide our time," Renna thought aloud.

"Exactly," Zandorn agreed. "We will leave the young

mage with the League. They will strengthen my instrument for me, and when the time comes, we will draw him out into the open and strike on our terms. There will be no room for error then," he said, narrowing his gaze towards Burvenin and Karazul. "Find the Druid, don't come back until you do." With that, he stood up and swiftly left the room.

Renna, Karazul, Burvenin, and Ymona sat in stillness for a few moments as Gunther moved around the table, pouring pemberry wine and clearing empty dishes that had been picked over during the meeting.

Burvenin was the first to move, piling extra food onto a plate before departing in uncharacteristic silence.

"He's going to be even *more* fun to work with now," Karazul lamented. "I don't get paid enough for this. Blast the damned blood contract his dark majesty made me sign."

"It was for a purpose, was it not?" Renna pointed out. "Isn't there something you need help locating?"

"*Someone*. My younger brother is not a thing," Karazul corrected.

"It's all a matter of perception," she observed.

"You lost your brother too?" Ymona asked.

Renna couldn't help but roll her eyes at Ymona's obvious ploy for an ally. When did Zandorn start attracting all these sad, family-starved souls?

Karazul nodded, continuing to manipulate the dagger in his hands. "Many lifetimes ago, it seems," he said softly. He flicked his eyes up from the dagger, flitting between the women, seeming to sharpen his thoughts.

"I wonder if Zandorn has even found my brother. It's

been years, and he's shared little more than an update in passing. Maybe I'd be better off searching on my own again..."

"Careful, Karazul. My father has ears everywhere," Renna warned.

"Now, now, you wouldn't betray me, would you?" Karazul's smile didn't reach his eyes.

"I won't have to," she warned again.

Chapter 18

TERASI

Terasi walked slowly and carefully through the forest, his dark green skin mirroring the tangled foliage around him. His worn robes dragged silently along the ground, heaving reluctantly forward as his bare feet pushed the tired fabric ahead with each step. An occasional ray of sunlight broke through the trees, catching his golden eyes and forcing him to squint. Whenever this happened, Terasi silently cursed the small antlers jutting from the top of his head, preventing him from wearing a hood to shield his eyes.

He plopped his staff down solidly on the ground, pausing to breathe deeply and survey his surroundings.

"Just as we thought, Elpida. Another mess of a forest," he muttered, looking down at his right shoulder.

There, a small, bronze-colored lizard sat with almost diligent attention. She looked up at Terasi and chirped in response to his voice—her fine scales ran from nose to tail, reflecting the light. She was no longer than the length of his hand from fingertip to wrist.

Terasi smiled at the creature and gently rubbed the bottom of her jaw with a single finger. Elpida closed her eyes and chirped again as he did so, apparently enjoying the attention.

"Thank you, friend," Terasi said. "You make an old Druid feel a little less alone."

Terasi turned his attention back to the forest, brow furrowing. As a Druid, his primary responsibility was to care for nature. Trees, plants, and wildlife often spoke to him when they needed help or purely for social matters. He remembered a particularly chatty oak tree with a penchant for puns. It had been decades since they last spoke, he realized.

He shuffled to the nearest tree and placed his palm on its trunk, closing his eyes to listen, begging the tree to offer some small message.

Nothing.

It was the same everywhere he went. Something disturbed these forests, his forests. Something took their voices. *No, not just their voices, their magic.* Their lifeblood. He slowly opened his eyes, gently patting the tree in silent understanding.

"This is why we need a Gathering, Elpida. A proper ritual with a few Druids could bring life back to these trees."

Elpida purred as she kneaded Terasi's shoulder, settling for an afternoon nap in the folds of his robe.

Terasi knew a Gathering would be complex, if not impossible. His fellow Druids all agreed over a century ago it was too dangerous to congregate. Once Zandorn's dark magic began infecting the world, the Druids couldn't risk being in one place. They knew Zandorn would catch them if he could and use them for his vile experiments. Besides, they now had too much work fighting the Rot that gripped Valecium. They needed to split up and cover as much ground as possible.

"Let's move on. Maybe there will be a few surviving trees up ahead."

Now fast asleep, Elpida wiggled slightly as the Druid began walking again.

As he moved through the forest, he sensed something disturbing. Usually, he could feel the forest, its magic and wildlife. It was a pleasant, warm buzzing in the back of his mind. Now, though, he sensed nothing. Life and magic were absent—there was no buzzing, only the quiet of death. He stopped and twitched his head to the side, listening. Feeling.

Something whistled through the air. He deftly ducked and rolled to safety, holding Elpida in one place on his shoulder as he did.

Three darts thudded against a tree, passing through the space his neck had been only moments ago.

He looked in the direction the darts had come from just in time to see silver flames pouring out of the woods, eating all the vegetation in its path.

Terasi jumped from his crouched position with an agility befitting someone much younger than he appeared. He clung to a tree nearly eight feet off the ground. He jumped from tree to tree, dodging another series of darts and jets of fire. He landed several lengths off the ground on a branch, stealing a glance below to identify his attackers.

A burly, muscular man burst through the shrubbery where the silver flames had been. More fire flowed from his hands, consuming the forest around him.

A low growl escaped Terasi's lips as he bared his teeth at the man. He dropped to a lower branch and moved toward the man to stop his destruction. As he did, a second attacker swung out from a tree on his left, connecting a foot solidly with Terasi's face.

He fell to the ground and rolled again, backward this time. Terasi righted himself, evaluating the second attacker. He was much smaller than the bigger man with the fire, but Terasi immediately feared him. This man—if he was a man—was the absence he had sensed earlier. It was like the man was nothing, a void in the world.

"You shouldn't try to speak with the trees, Moss-Eater," the bigger man shouted. "This one will track you every time." He gestured to the smaller man.

"Who are you?" Terasi asked. "Why do you destroy my forest? What have you done to these trees?"

"None of that is important," said the smaller man. He was smiling, but it wasn't from joy. The expression reminded Terasi of predators he had observed right before a kill. A quiet, terrifying confidence. "If you must know, my name is Karazul, and my partner here is Burvenin. We've been looking for you for a long time. You're coming with us," he said, stepping forward.

"You're Zandorn's men," Terasi said, answering his own question. It made sense—he had heard whispers from the earth of disturbances in many forests. It was intentional, me-thodic, as if someone was looking for something. Now he knew that Zandorn was looking for Druids.

Without a word, Karazul launched himself forward, simultaneously drawing one of his blades. Vines snapped down to wrap around his arm, catching him in midair. They yanked and twisted his body, throwing him back to slam against a tree.

Terasi stood unmoving, settling his gaze on Burvenin with a silent challenge.

Burvenin took the bait, throwing several fireballs at Terasi.

The Druid ducked and snaked around each one, landing softly back on the ground. The fire hit trees and plants behind Terasi and burst into flames. With a gesture he quieted the fires as if they had never been.

Burvenin snarled and moved his arms in several complex gestures. A wall of earth rose behind Terasi, cutting off his escape route. Dozens of smaller spikes of stone erupted from the ground near his sides, closing in.

Terasi again stood, unmoving. "I haven't fought anyone in many years," he said calmly. "A result of my isolation." He glanced down at Elpida to check on her.

The bronze lizard was alert, crouching low and baring her fangs. While they were quite small, Terasi knew from experience they were sharper than most blades.

He looked back to Burvenin, who was visibly confused that his stone spikes and earth wall had ceased moving. Terasi glanced at the structures, smirking.

"I know it wouldn't be wise to prolong this fight, especially being outnumbered," Terasi said. "Yet it is you at the disadvantage."

"How's that now?" Burvenin shouted. His eyes darted,

still puzzling out why his spells stopped.

"I assume I'm the first Druid you've encountered," Terasi said, an almost playful lilt in his voice.

Was he enjoying this a little? Or maybe he was excited at the prospect of a small amount of justice for his desecrated forests.

"There are two things you should know." Terasi gently set his staff down on the ground in front of him. "The first is that we Druids draw power from the forests around us."

He unclasped his robe, carefully lifted Elpida, and placed her on the ground in the middle of the fabric next to his staff. He muttered a few words, and a small, green sphere appeared around the bronze lizard, a rather strong defensive enchantment to protect the creature. He couldn't risk her getting hurt in this mess.

As he stood, now without his robes covering his upper body, the runes and tattoos rippled across his green skin, all of varying hues and textures. While he wasn't overly muscular, his frame was lithe and wiry with evident strength.

Burvenin's eyes widened in shock as thorns and bark sprouted from Terasi's skin, covering him in protective armor. He looked more like a walking tree than anything at this point.

"The second thing you should know," Terasi continued, "is that you've decided to attack me in one of the largest forests on the continent." He locked eyes with Burvenin and placed a hand on the earthen wall behind him. The entire structure crumbled in less than a second as if it were made of sand.

Thick vines shot from the treetops, wrapping around Burvenin's arms and legs. They kept coming, creating a makeshift cocoon, slithering up, down, and around the man's body to cover him completely.

Karazul regained his footing and went for Terasi again, blades whipping so fast they were almost invisible.

Terasi dodged most of the swipes with inhuman agility but wasn't quick enough to escape unscathed. Minor nicks chipped away at the bark and thorn armor covering his arms and torso. As he worked his way out of Karazul's range, a well-timed blade moving upward caught his shoulder and lifted him off his feet. He landed hard on his back, an unnatural fall for the Druid.

Karazul advanced, and Terasi crawled back a few feet, slamming the ground with a fist. A crack formed, stretching from his fist toward Karazul's feet, and swallowed the man's left leg up to his knee. Karazul snarled in frustration.

Terasi stood and turned in time to see Burvenin incinerating his vine-wrapped prison from the inside out, shedding the scorched encasing and stumbling toward him.

He quickly surveyed his surroundings. More than a dozen trees were fully or partially burned, the forest floor was torn up from various spells, and several new fires were about to catch from Burvenin's latest magic.

Terasi was confident in his magic, especially in this forest, but the damage this skirmish had already caused was too great a price to pay. He couldn't be responsible for any more destruction in his forest. He needed to lead the attackers away and hope he could defeat them near the edges of his forest.

Terasi stepped back and melted into a tree, disappearing.

Karazul, one leg still trapped in the earth beneath him, had thrown a dagger the second the Druid twitched with movement. It sank into the tree halfway to the hilt and stopped abruptly. He howled a primitive yell.

"Vexing leaf slime," Burvenin cursed. He offered a hand to Karazul, who took it and pulled himself out of the small hole in the ground. "Expel him from the tree!"

"He's moved on. We'll need to find him again," Karazul explained. He could sense the Druid's magic taking him further and further from their current location. "It should be easier now we've forced him to use bigger magic."

"Weeks of tracking, and you fumble the first encounter. Brilliant work, really," Burvenin huffed.

"At least I made contact. You just set everything ablaze and pick through the remnants. You should take a lesson in finesse."

Burvenin grumbled. "Let's get this over with. I'll send word to Renna and Kalbick to join us. Start tracking."

CHAPTER 19
REAL STORIES

Zak was meditating—or trying to—on an expansive second-floor communal balcony in the Dormitory. It was late afternoon, and the hint of cool evening air layered into the gentle breeze brushing his face.

He wasn't a typical acolyte, but sleeping in the dorms felt as close as he'd get. He politely declined Sorwin's offer to stay at his family's townhouse. Zak trusted Sorwin now—after everything, how could he not? But he needed a little time and space for himself to think.

Zak sat cross-legged, trying not to be annoyed by his distracting, drifting thoughts. It had been almost a week since he activated the *indagomius* and something else within him. He couldn't shake the image of his arms covered in green scales and long, black claws instead of fingers. What *was* that?

He asked Sorwin that very question countless times in the last few days. Unfortunately, *Nacusti* were exceedingly rare, and his bloodline was the only one known to still exist. Sorwin, and even Tansil, with his long elven lifespan, had little experience with *Nacusti* magic. It's not like he had any blood relatives around to ask, either.

As best as Zak could understand, from what he pieced together from Sorwin and Tansil, he had two magics within him: his own, natural magic, and that of the Guardian that was gifted to his ancestor, Adrastus Belcour, and passed down through each generation. One working theory of Tansil's was that the Guardian magic overwhelmed Zak when he tapped into it when powering the *indagomius,* causing a partial transformation. Zak couldn't help but wonder what would have happened if he kept going. What would he have turned into?

The sound of steps approaching from behind interrupted his thoughts. As he opened his eyes, he looked up to see Olivia standing in front of him, casually leaning on the nearby railing of the balcony. While her posture was relaxed, Zak saw ferocity in her eyes. They searched his face, reminding him of a look Kal would get when he was determined to solve a puzzle. Was Zak a puzzle to her?

"You ready?" she asked, still staring intently at him.

Zak let a small sigh escape. "Maybe. I'm not sure if I'm up for it today."

Once Zak had recovered from his transformation at the healing wards, he requested to resume his studies in offensive and defensive magics. Somehow, Sorwin had convinced Euphemius to let Olivia spar with Zak for an hour each afternoon.

"Not in the mood for more bruises?" Olivia smirked, but her eyes still fixated on Zak, still searching.

"Not really," he said, stretching and wincing slightly as he stood. It was true—Olivia had given him a proper thrashing while sparring the last two days.

Olivia frowned. "Look, *Nacusti,* this isn't charity. I'm supposed to teach you how to survive in a fight. Let's go." As she said the last part, she flicked her wrist, and a small force hit Zak's shoulder, pushing him back a step.

Zak was usually a patient person, but he was in no mood for this today. He had too much on his mind, and his body felt exhausted anyway. What really irked him, though, was how Olivia addressed him.

"Don't call me *Nacusti*," he said. He turned his back to her, walking away on the long stone balcony toward the door.

"Why not?" she called after him, followed by another magical push. This time, Zak stumbled a few steps forward.

Heat welled up inside him, anger flushing as he turned on his heel to face her. "STOP!" he shouted, feeling his eyes widen.

"Try to make me, *Nacusti*," she countered with a devious smile.

Zak lost any grasp on logic or patience and launched himself forward, angling a right hook for Olivia's jaw. She deftly leaned back and pushed his weight behind him, making him stumble again.

Without stopping, Zak kept his momentum going by twisting into a turn and launching a kick at her midsection. Again, she jumped back just out of his reach.

"Why does it bother you, being called what you are, *Nacusti*?" she jeered.

Zak moved in again with a flurry of attacks, each deflected

or dodged.

"Because," Zak said through gritted teeth, still furiously trying to land even a single blow. "I'm sick of it! Sick of hearing about my heritage and powers when I can't even control them!"

As Olivia danced out of range again, Zak switched to magic. He pulled on his power, throwing streams of emerald fire at his opponent. She dodged some of the fire, and some she deflected with her hand. Olivia was annoyingly good at fighting, Zak had learned. She still had the same devious smile on her face.

"You're right," she said over the blare of the fire, "you really can't control your magic at all."

Zak made a hoarse noise—half yell, half grunt—and pulled his hands together to form one large spout of fire, funneling it toward Olivia.

Olivia widened her stance and met his emerald fire with her amber-hued flames. It felt like a solid force when their flames met, like pushing against a wall that wouldn't move.

Zak could barely see Olivia on the other side of the fire, but he could tell she wasn't smiling anymore. Her face looked more serious or perhaps taut with effort.

Good. He was finally getting to her, it seemed.

He pushed harder, letting his anger fuel his magic. He felt the fire grow larger and larger. It began whipping around Olivia's amber flames, pushing the spout closer to where she stood.

Then suddenly, there was no resistance. Zak's flames shot through the air and hit the stone of the balcony floor, instantly blackening the surface. He stopped, confused, and a fist connected solidly with his gut, knocking the wind out of him. He fell backward, landing hard and gasping for air.

Still coughing, he managed a glance up to see Olivia standing above him, face hardened. Somehow, she had released her spell and snuck up right in front of him.

"We don't get to choose who we're born, Zak. But we can choose who we become." She stood, staring at him with a steely gaze. Her stillness was unnerving.

As his breath slowly steadied, he grunted and stood.

"What do you know about who I've been born? I might have family out there I've never even met—maybe I never will. They're probably dead. That's how I ended up in Densba in the first place!" His anger rose again, and his voice grew louder. Zak returned her stare with his own.

"You're not the only one with a story in this city, you know." Olivia's voice was quiet and even. "Everyone has their own history following them."

The words flew out of his mouth before he knew what he was saying. "What kind of history could you possibly have? Sorwin said you're an orphan too."

Olivia's whole body tensed, and Zak thought she would kill him. He also thought he might deserve it, immediately regretting what he said.

"Olivia...I'm sorry, I didn't—" he started.

"Don't," she said. "Don't speak of things you know nothing about." Even though her voice was almost a whisper, Zak clearly heard the fury in her tone.

"I'm sorry," he said again. "I'm sorry you lost them...I..."

He didn't know what to say.

"I didn't lose them!" she yelled, turning and walking a few steps to brace herself on the railing.

Zak hesitated, frozen where he stood. He was coming down from his anger-fueled tantrum, and guilt quickly took over. He slowly walked to the railing, also resting his hands on it, looking over the field below. He felt he shouldn't look at Olivia for some reason, even though she was less than an arm's length away.

She took a few shaky breaths before she spoke again. "I had parents. We lived on a small farm to the northwest of here. We didn't have much, and when my magic started manifesting, it was out of control. I'd reach for something only to have it burn to ashes in my hand. Or while shoveling in the field, the very earth beneath my feet changed to muddy water."

Olivia was staring straight down, her knuckles turning white as she gripped the rough stone railing tight.

"With that kind of power, I was terrified to even be near my parents. What would happen if I hugged them? Or looked at them too long? I started sleeping in the barn, and we traded what we could for magic lessons. Sometimes room and board for a traveling mage would buy me a spell or technique to try and control my magic. But nothing worked for long. I destroyed things left and right, causing my parents to lose more than we made. One night, I had a nightmare and woke up to the entire barn engulfed in flames. That's when I knew what I had to do. I was seven when I ran away."

A heavy silence filled the space between Zak and Olivia. He couldn't imagine the burden and guilt she felt. Though, perhaps he could. He felt a pang each time he thought of Kal, how he was responsible for his misfortune. He wondered if Olivia felt the same about her parents.

Zak's face scrunched. "I'm so sorry, Olivia. I had no idea."

"Of course you didn't. That's the point," she said quickly, turning to him. "That look on your face? That's what I hate the most. The pity. It's easier to be an orphan. At least it's straightforward. People can understand that story. The girl with power oozing out of her to the point she destroyed her home and almost killed her parents daily? That's complicated, messy."

"What happened?" Zak asked softly. "After you ran away, I mean. How'd you end up here?"

Olivia shrugged. "I wandered through forests and a few villages, begging or trying to work for food when I could. Usually, within a few days, I'd destroy something or nearly kill someone. Eventually, Sorwin found me and brought me here, trained me."

Zak had a lot more questions but thought he saw Olivia's cheeks redden for a moment, though he couldn't be sure. He watched as she seemed to search for words.

"I'm sorry," she said, and that surprised him. "I've been pushing you since I met you. First, I pushed you away, and now I'm pushing you to work hard because I understand you. I think...I think our stories, our real stories, are similar. Except yours is out there for everyone to know, and my shame and fear hide mine."

"You can't blame yourself, not for any of it," Zak said. He tried to change his expression to be more assertive, relaxed, or anything besides what he imagined it to be, the one Olivia didn't like. "You were a kid, and no one could have expected you to deal with that power on your own."

"And neither can you," Olivia said flatly but softly, looking up into his eyes. "I learned control eventually, and you will too. I'll even help you." She smiled, maybe the first genuine smile Zak had seen on her face.

He couldn't help but smile back, looking down at her, noticing how nicely her auburn curls framed her face.

Before he could say anything, she gently elbowed him. Her genuine smile shifted into the practiced, joking smile he had become very familiar with. "C'mon, let's go check on the *indagomius*. You have to refill it again, right?"

Zak nodded. "Every few days, according to Tansil."

"Think you have enough magic left after that fit you pitched?"

Zak rolled his eyes, not taking the bait this time. "Guess we'll find out," he said as they set off toward Tansil's office.

CHAPTER 20

SET IN MOTION

Zak climbed the many stairs up to Tansil's tower office. When he reached the top, he knocked on the large wooden doors. He paused, listening for a response, but heard none.

Olivia moved up the last few steps and stood behind him. Zak turned to her and shrugged.

"Seems Tansil isn't here," he said.

"We can wait just inside," Olivia offered. She pushed through the office doors and waved him in.

Zak followed, looking around the windowed room. He hadn't been back here since his last encounter with the *indagomius* when he lost control and started changing.

"Let's get this over with," Zak said, his voice cracking slightly. He moved toward the *indagomius* to place it on the floor.

"Shouldn't we wait?" Olivia asked.

"Why?" He turned toward Olivia, her brow furrowed. Was that concern he saw?

"Well, last time...it didn't go well, did it?" Her tone was

more of a statement than a question.

Zak's chest tightened. "It won't be like last time, Olivia. It won't need as much magic." His frustration crept up again. *Maybe that will help,* he thought, imagining the fuel the emotion would give his fire.

"Are you sure?" She asked again. "Tansil will most likely be—"

"I said I can do this!" Zak yelled. He *needed* to be able to do this. If he couldn't do something as simple as pouring magic into an object, what hope did he have of defeating the Consortium, or Zandorn, or saving Kal?

Olivia put her hands up, yielding. "Alright, I'll be here if you need." She took a few steps back and folded her arms, watching him.

Zak turned back to the *indagomius* and took a deep breath. Just as he was about to reach for it, the purple gem floated from its spot on the table and started flashing a bright, white light. Then, a loud blaring sound began emitting from the gold frame around the *indagomius*. It was like a horn Zak had heard at a parade in his hometown.

"What in the Three Fires does that mean?" Zak managed to yell above the blaring. He squinted against the bright light and covered his ears to shut out the noise. Olivia was barely visible through the light, and he could just make out her hunched shape, trying similar tactics.

In a brief moment of eye contact, Zak saw her mouth moving but couldn't hear the words through the blaring of the *indagomius.*

"I'm going to grab it to see if I can stop it," Zak yelled to

Olivia, though he doubted she could hear him either.

He moved toward the purple gem, trying not to look directly at it for fear of going completely blind. In between flashes of light, he pinpointed its exact location on the table. Memorizing the spot and closing his eyes, his hand darted for the *indagomius*. The flashing and blaring immediately stopped after he grabbed it.

"Finally," Zak let out a relieved sigh, his eyes still closed. "Are you okay?"

When he opened his eyes, turning to where Olivia should have been standing, she wasn't there. Or rather, *he* wasn't there.

Zak was no longer in Tansil's office.

He was standing in the middle of a forest.

Sorwin flipped through the papers in front of him that detailed the latest scouting reports from the field. He was in a council meeting with the other League leaders, but he didn't want to be. He didn't feel he needed to be here. He needed to be training Zak, preparing him for the inevitable conflict ahead. His fingers drummed on the large, octagonal table, betraying his impatience.

As General Lupa concluded recounting the information from the scouting report, the door to the council chambers burst open. Heads snapped toward the entrance from the loud echo of the doors slamming against the walls.

Olivia was running toward the council, two guards

sprawled on the floor behind her. Apparently, they didn't admit her to the chambers willingly.

"Olivia!" Euphemius shouted, his eyes darting between his charge and the guards in her wake, still regaining their footing. "How dare you—"

"Zakolor is gone!" she shouted back, still somewhat breathless from her sprint and scuffle with the guards.

A gasp rippled through the council. Sorwin couldn't breathe at all.

"Gone? What do you mean gone?" Vermig asked.

Olivia looked to Tansil, who had stood in his surprise. "It was the *indagomius*. We went to refill it, but it made all these noises and lights and Zak grabbed it to stop it, but then he was gone."

Horror gripped Olivia. She usually looked older than her age, more mature. Seeing her now, Sorwin remembered how young she truly was.

He turned to Tansil. "It's done, yes? The *indagomius* found the Druid and took Zak there?"

Tansil nodded. "It happened sooner than expected. I thought we had more time to prepare him." The elf dug in a pocket at his waist, pulling out a small stone that was the same hue as the *indagomius*.

"This will lead you to the *indagomius*," Tansil continued. "Pray that our young *Nacusti* kept the other stone with him."

Sorwin took the matching stone from Tansil and turned to leave, striding only a few paces before a voice interrupted him.

"Wait!" Vermig shouted, his strong voice piercing the

confusion in the room.

Sorwin paused, sighed deeply, and turned. "With all due respect, Archalium, waiting is *exactly* what I cannot do at this moment. Zakolor is somewhere in the world, alone and vulnerable. We need to move now if we have any hope of finding him before Zandorn."

"You and Tansil got him in this mess, and you expect the rest of us to stand idly by, letting you muck it up again?" Vermig countered. "No, not this time. Your Highness." Vermig addressed Marius. "I believe this rescue mission is too large a responsibility to leave to one house. Both myself and Archlumen Sashina should each send a representative with Sorwin."

"And I'd send one as well," General Lupa said. "You magic houses often forget it's the military that keeps our borders safe. We deserve a representative on the mission."

Sorwin sighed again, watching High King Marius evaluate the situation. His advisor, Limba Dar, leaned down to whisper in the king's ear. Another moment passed before Marius spoke.

"Motion granted. The Archalium, leader of the Den of Darkness, Archlumen, leader of Temple of Light, and General Lupa will each assign one of their numbers to accompany Sorwin to rescue the *Nacusti*."

"She'll be going as well," Euphemius said flatly, gesturing to Olivia. "She needs to fix this mess she helped create."

Sorwin nodded, not opposed to the extra help but feeling the acute pressure of time. "Yes, fine. Have each of your selected representatives meet me at the western stable within half an hour. We haven't a moment to spare." He turned and quickly left the room, Olivia trailing a step behind him.

Time moved fast. Sorwin and Olivia had just enough to stop by his townhouse and pull together as many necessities as they could.

Olivia grabbed a large pack and threw in pieces of bread, fruits, and anything that looked remotely edible. Without knowing how long they'd be gone, it was best to prepare for anything.

Sorwin went to his study, quickly scanning his shelves and pulling a few books and several magical artifacts. It was difficult preparing for the unknown. Though he had done it many times, it never seemed to get easier.

Now, the two stood outside the large stable on the western side of Tor'alan. The timber frame building had a wide and tall opening, and the doors flung open almost permanently with the constant in-and-out traffic.

Bazil approached the pair, a severe look on his face and a small pack bouncing at his waist.

"I lobbied with Archlumen Sashina as soon as I heard," he said to Sorwin once he was within earshot. "I may have mentioned my experience with our *Nacusti's*...previous episode."

"Glad to have you," Sorwin said. "If we encounter trouble, a priest like yourself will be invaluable."

"More like '*when* we encounter trouble' with you, Sorwin." A full voice cut through the throng of the stable square.

Sorwin turned to his right, though he already knew the speaker.

"Shira Motchit, I never dreamed I'd be so lucky," Sorwin smiled at his old friend. "How in the Three Fires did you convince Vermig to let you come?"

Shira was a short and wide woman who waddled more than walked. She had a big smile on her face, never able to contain her personality, even in the face of danger.

"That old *stulmati* owes me more than a few favors. Besides, one of my demons is the best tracker in the League. You'll be needing him, I hear."

Sorwin nodded as he shook Shira's hand. "Undoubtedly we will, especially if Zak doesn't have the *indagomius* on him."

Another man jogged up to the growing group. He set down a pack with a sword strapped to it on the ground next to him.

"Major Kaleb Deidaku, reporting in," the man said. He was tall, nearly as tall as Sorwin, with a strong jaw, black hair, and matching dark eyes. Sorwin couldn't help but feel a slight flutter just at the sight of him.

"So you are," he said, perhaps more coyly than intended. He nodded and refocused, knowing the rush they were in. He facilitated introductions for the group, as most did not know one another.

"Right, let's get to it. You have all heard the situation. Our task is to find Zakolor as fast as possible and bring him back here. Secondarily, the *indagomius* should have taken Zak close or directly to a Druid. If we happen across the Druid, we should attempt to communicate and convince them to return to Tor'alan with us as well. Questions?"

"Any known threats in the area?" Kaleb asked.

"None that we're aware of recently, though I'd expect Zandorn to continue to be a step ahead of us. He may have sensed or tracked the magic from the *indagomius*."

"Has Zak's training...um, progressed?" Bazil asked, perhaps attempting tact.

Olivia piped in. "It has, actually. We've been sparring nonstop the last few days. He's improved rather quickly and gained more control."

Bazil nodded his understanding.

"How are we traveling?" Shira asked.

Sorwin smiled. "I'm so glad you asked, dear Shira. We'll be flying, of course. It's the quickest direct line to Zak's location."

Olivia, Bazil, and Kaleb's eyes widened as they shared a few confused glances. Shira chuckled rather loudly.

"You do know you're the only one here who can fly, Sorwin?" Bazil offered.

"Ah! Yes, of course. Well, Shira has a few demons she could use if preferred. But for the rest of you, you'll need some assistance. This way!" He started off at a brisk pace into the stables.

The group gathered their things and quickly followed.

"Do we have flying horses now?" Olivia asked. Sorwin detected mostly sarcasm in her voice, though perhaps a hint of hope.

"Nothing quite so elegant, no," he answered. "Not everything in this stable is equine."

As he finished his sentence, the group rounded a corner and froze, staring up at a pair of giant beasts.

"It would appear you're right," Bazil said, blanching.

CHAPTER 21
MEETINGS

Zak blinked in confusion, standing in the middle of a forest. He looked down, his hand still clutching the *indagomius*. At least the blaring and bright flashing light had stopped.

Did it work? Did the *indagomius* bring him to a Druid?

He put the gem into a pocket and looked around. It was late afternoon, and the light was fading into a darker shade of orange. The forest's edge was up ahead, and so was a clearing beyond the line of trees. Zak paused to listen but couldn't hear any birds or animals. A soft breeze rustled the leaves on nearby trees, but all else was silent.

Unnaturally silent.

Zak stepped toward the clearing to look for landmarks and figure out where the *indagomius* had dropped him. As soon as he moved, a vine shot up from the earth and wrapped around his entire body. It happened so fast that all he could do was gasp before he was immobilized.

The vine stopped at his shoulders, leaving his neck and head free.

"Who are you?" a voice asked from behind.

Zak tried to twist to see the speaker, but the vines tightened with every movement, and he winced at the strain on his body. He needed to think, to buy himself time.

"I'm Zak. Who are you?" he grunted.

"How did you find me? What are you doing here?" the voice asked.

"I answered your first question. How about answering one of mine?" Zak countered, still squirming.

A moment passed before quiet footsteps sounded on the forest floor. A tall figure with green skin and antlers moved in front of Zak, golden eyes peering down at his captive.

"You...you're the Druid!" Zak exclaimed. He was in awe of the figure standing in front of him. He couldn't believe it, the *indagomius* had worked!

"A Druid, not *the* Druid," the green figure corrected Zak. "I am Terasi. How did you find me? What are you doing here?"

"I'm with the League of Kingdoms. We've been looking for you to warn you and offer protection. Zandorn is after you," Zak explained. So many thoughts rushed through his mind he started speaking faster.

"I know," Terasi responded calmly. "I'm handling them. What are you doing here?"

"We came to help you, to intercept the Consortium. They took my friend, and I'm trying to get him back."

"We? You're alone. How did you find me?" Terasi repeated. His eyes scanned the forest behind Zak.

"I..." Zak was caught off guard by Terasi's directness.

"It was supposed to be a group of us. I muddled the plan a bit." He stared at the ground, his jaw tightening. He couldn't afford any mistakes—any *more* mistakes—not when he was finally getting closer to Kal.

"I used an *indagomius*," Zak said, staring defiantly up at Terasi. He decided to tell the Druid whatever he could. He needed to gain his trust.

That caught Terasi's attention as his eyes darted down to Zak.

"An *indagomius*? That is old magic, *Parignis*."

Zak's brow furrowed, recalling his recent studies of ancient language to translate what Terasi had called him.

"Little fire? What does that mean?" Zak asked, bristling. He didn't know the meaning, but it sounded like an insult.

Terasi's mouth twitched into a slight smirk—something Zak didn't think the stern Druid was capable of—as the vines slowly receded.

Zak gently rolled his shoulders and stretched, shaking off the soreness from the tight vines.

"It's an old term for young mages. Our people used to be close, you know. Or would you prefer *Nacusti* instead?"

Zak froze. "How did you know?" he asked, his body tensing reflexively.

"My kind can find me without an *indagomius*, so they would have no use for such a thing. *Nacusti* magic is the only kind still around that would work. Plus, you smell of Guardian."

"Smell?"

Terasi tilted his head. "Did they not teach you this in your college, *Nacusti?*"

"Don't call me that," Zak said, sharper than he intended. "Please."

Terasi looked down his nose at Zak. "Very well, *Parignis*. We should move. Zandorn's men will be here soon, and I cannot fight them and protect you at the same time."

"I can help. You know about the *Nacusti*, which means you know what I can do."

"*Nacusti* or no, you are still a *Parignis*. You will only get in the way," Terasi responded coolly.

Zak grunted, restraining his temper. "Look, I'm sure Tansil and Sorwin will send someone after me when they hear I'm gone, which means we'll get help soon. All we have to do is hold the Consortium off long enough for them to arrive."

"That is more of a hope than a plan, but it seems you will get your wish," Terasi said. "They're here."

Zak followed the direction Terasi gestured with a nod. A few dozen yards away, two figures emerged from the treeline into the clearing.

Zak's heart jumped as he saw the figures. There was no mistake—he had seen them both before. Burvenin and Karazul sauntered into the middle of the clearing.

He wasn't sure who he expected Zandorn to send after the Druid, but he should have known it would be these two. Burvenin started this whole mess by kidnapping Kal, and Karazul had dogged his every step to Tor'alan.

Zak's fists clenched and opened several times, his weight shifting between his feet.

"You know them?" Terasi said more than asked. "Good,

then you understand our situation."

"I may be a *Parignis* to you, but I learn fast," Zak countered. "I can buy time by keeping Burvenin busy if you can handle Karazul."

Terasi leaned back for a moment, evaluating Zak. "Perhaps you are smarter than you look. Very well, but the world would be darker without the *Nacusti* in it. Try not to die."

As Terasi moved toward the clearing, Zak fell in step right beside the Druid. His entire body felt like it was on fire, burning with nervous energy. His stomach twisted in knots, and his heart pounded through his ears with every step. He felt as if he was moving closer to Kal by confronting his kidnapper.

"I'm coming, Kal," he whispered.

Zak and Terasi stopped a fair distance from Burvenin and Karazul but close enough that Zak could see the lines of their faces, their hard and confident expressions. Karazul stood motionless with his blades drawn as Burvenin cracked his knuckles in his palms.

"It must be our lucky day, Karazul. The two prizes we've chased around the world happen to be in the same field at the same time!" Burvenin jeered, a wicked smile baring his teeth.

"This is your chance to fix your previous blunder, Burvenin. Don't let the *Nacusti* evade you a second time," Karazul shot back. His eyes never strayed from Terasi, like he had found his prey and couldn't look away.

Terasi remained still, though Zak could tell the Druid's entire body was tense and ready to spring into action.

"If you have a weapon, now might be the time to produce it, *Parignis*," Terasi said quietly.

Zak nodded and reached for his magic, quieting his mind as much as he could, pushing his anxiety and fear back to the corners of his thoughts.

"*Anima mea telum*," Zak said, weaving his arms in a circular pattern before stretching them apart. As he did, a dark wooden staff with an emerald stone at the top manifested in his grip.

He could hear Burvenin's booming laugh. "Seems you've learned a few tricks, *Nacusti*! This might actually be fun."

Zak said nothing but tightened his grip on the staff. He couldn't sort through the flood of emotions fast enough for a response. It was too late, anyway, as Karazul launched himself toward Terasi.

Vines immediately sprang from the earth in Karazul's path, attempting to wrap around his legs. He deftly wove between them, slicing the few that managed to get near him.

Terasi jumped back, putting more space between him and Karazul.

Zak gasped as Karazul ran right past him without even a glance in his direction. The assassin was so focused on his prey that he couldn't be bothered to divert his attention. Zak couldn't believe the incredible speed with which Karazul moved.

Before he could appreciate the dangerous battle to his right, he saw a flicker of movement ahead. A wave of water crashed into him, lifting him off his feet. He spun and twisted several times before the water dispersed, leaving him coughing and drenched on the ground.

Zak inhaled as deep as he could, trying to catch his breath

as he regained his footing. He heard Burvenin laughing again.

"You've caused me a lot of trouble, *Nacusti*," he said. With a gesture, Burvenin sent another stream of water flying toward Zak.

Zak planted his staff in the ground and pushed as much magic as he could into his spell. "*Tegoperignis!*"

A torrent of emerald fire wrapped itself around him. The stream of water hit his shield hard, violently hissing as it evaporated. He knew fire wasn't a good defense for water magic, but his reflexes took over in the moment. Luckily, his shield was holding for now.

Again, Zak heard Burvenin's laugh. He hated that barking sound and his fists tightened in anger as the mage slowly walked closer to him.

"Seems you have some strong fire, *Nacusti*. So do I," Burvenin snarled.

As he did, he raised his hands, and silver fire erupted from his palms, crashing into Zak's emerald shield.

Zak grunted. The force of Burvenin's fire was unbelievably strong. His feet slipped under the weight as the silver flames pushed down on his magic.

This is bad. He couldn't hold his shield under this kind of pressure for long. The colliding flames blared loud as they whipped around, and Zak could barely hear himself think.

"Is this all you have, *Nacusti*? I saw more fight in Kalbick than this."

Zak's eyes widened at the sound of Kal's name coming out of *his* mouth. He could barely see Burvenin's face through the inferno, but he saw enough of the man to glare in his direction.

Zak yelled, feeling the logical part of him fall away, replaced by instinct. It was as if all the anger and guilt he had carried since losing Kal took over in an instant.

The emerald shield around Zak started rotating faster and faster. The speed deflected Burvenin's fire quicker, lessening the pressure. With another yell, Zak pushed himself forward into a jog, then a run, toward Burvenin, closing the distance between them. His shield moved with him, splitting Burvenin's fire down the middle.

A few feet in front of the mage, Zak stopped and thrust his staff forward. His green flames unwrapped and swallowed Burvenin's silver flames, shooting toward the bigger man.

Both spells exploded as they impacted on Burvenin.

Zak waited for a moment, a cloud of smoke blocking his vision. It thinned, and as it did, he saw Burvenin standing with a wall of stone around him. He was unharmed and still smiling at Zak as if taunting him.

"Not bad, *Nacusti*. Not bad at all," Burvenin said, brushing some ash off his clothes. "You have good instincts when you listen to them."

"Where is Kal?" Zak yelled. "What have you done with him?"

"Oh, you'll be reunited with your friend soon. He's on his way here."

"What?" Zak said, breathless.

Before he could say anything else, Burvenin stomped on the ground with his foot. A chunk of earth a few feet in front of Zak launched itself up, slamming into his gut. He wheezed and fell hard on his back, the wind leaving his body and forcing him to cough again.

Zak rolled to his side, clutching his stomach and trying to breathe. He looked up to see Burvenin and his infuriating, toothy smile.

"What do you mean Kal is coming here?" Zak asked, wincing as he slowly regained his footing.

Burvenin didn't seem to be in a hurry to kill or capture him, Zak noted. The mage had several opportunities to do either, but he kept letting Zak get back up. He didn't know why, but that was becoming useful to buy time.

"Kalbick serves Zandorn now. Your friend is coming to collect you," Burvenin said.

Zak's stomach dropped. It felt similar to when he twisted through the Tor'alan portal, except a thousand times worse. His breath was shallow, almost stopping entirely. Thoughts muddied by confusion and rage bounced in his head. How was it possible Kal served Zandorn? The Consortium? Kal was the one who wanted to join the war to *stop* the Consortium.

"You're lying," Zak said flatly. Glancing down, he saw green crawling around his hands and up his arms.

Ah, you returned, the voice said.

Zak was losing control. Was this Burvenin's plan? Did he know this could happen? Zak didn't care—all he could think of was Kal, and Burvenin's taunts, and that made him angrier.

"I'm not lying. You'll see soon enough." Burvenin's eyes narrowed as he noticed the green moving up Zak's arms. "What's this? A new trick?"

Let's show him.

Zak loosed a guttural yell. He was faster than before, throwing a flurry of strikes with his staff at Burvenin.

The older mage parried a few attacks with his hands. Zak connected one solid hit across Burvenin's cheek. Both Zak and Burvenin paused, seemingly both in shock that Zak landed a hit.

Burvenin finally dropped his smile, replacing it with a scowl as he wiped a spot of blood where the staff connected. Apparently, he didn't enjoy losing the upper hand in the battle.

"You'll pay for that one, *Nacusti*," Burvenin promised. His hands began glowing with silver flames.

Zak didn't wait to see the mage's spell.

"*Ignis!*" Zak yelled, pointing his staff toward Burvenin.

Emerald flames erupted from the gem at the tip. The torrent of fire met Burvenin's silver flames once again, the two spouts fighting for dominance.

You can do more, the voice said, deep and rumbling. *You need to, to live.*

"You're not wrong," Zak said, knowing he couldn't hold his ground against Burvenin for long, not in a real fight.

Zak reached deeper, pulling as much magic as he could, and channeled it into his flames. The spout tripled in size and strength, pushing Burvenin's flames back closer and closer to his hands.

As he did, the green sped further up Zak's arms. He could feel it now, the change. It was racing up his neck and down his torso. Scales sprouted along his arms too.

His vision started changing. He saw things more clearly, with more detail. Colors shifted as well, objects taking on a glow of some kind. His magic was brighter, more defined. He could actually see Burvenin's face through the tempest of fire magic.

What in the Three Fires is happening?

Now you can see, can't you? said the voice.

Zak's mind started splitting. Part of him was utterly confused and wanted to ask hundreds of questions. Another part of him wanted to embrace this new power and use it to rescue his friend.

"What else can we do?" Zak asked aloud, hoping the voice could hear him.

Use more magic to find out, said the voice.

Zak widened his stance, pushing even more energy into his spell. He was barely aware of the grunts escaping him as he felt more changes ripple throughout his body. He was focused solely on defeating Burvenin by any means necessary.

The emerald fire pushed further and overwhelmed Burvenin. With his new sight, Zak saw the flash of fear on Burvenin's face. This time, the flames erupted on Burvenin, and Zak knew the spell had made contact. The mage's body flew backward several lengths and skid to a stop.

Zak breathed heavily, the exertion of magic catching up with him. He looked down, and his hands had wholly transformed, entirely covered in green scales, and where his fingernails used to be were arched black claws. Looking further down, he saw his feet had burst through his boots. They were longer and more slender, with scales and claws that matched his hands.

He didn't have time to think, to be scared of what was happening to his body. He saw Burvenin moving already, getting up again.

Zak didn't need to buy time anymore. Now, with this new power, he wanted to finish this quickly.

CHAPTER 22

REUNIONS

Sorwin blazed through the sky at frightening speed, his golden brown wings cutting through the air. He flew just above and slightly behind the rest of his companions, keeping a watchful eye as they clung to the backs of two wyverns.

The beasts were like giant flying lizards, slender but muscular bodies covered in surprisingly smooth scales. Each was a blueish-brown mottled hue. Their long necks and tails made both flying and swimming easy. Leathery wings beat the air as their large, orblike eyes scanned the horizon.

Convincing Olivia to ride one of the beasts was a feat, though he imagined it was more manageable given the guilt she harbored over Zak's predicament. She escorted him to the *indagomius* and was there when the gem whisked him into the middle of somewhere.

Sorwin knew Olivia shouldn't feel guilty that Zak decided to grasp the gem. Yet he also knew thoughts and feelings were often far from logical. It may even be that he and Tansil shared most of the responsibility for the situation, failing to explain the plan and how the indagomius functioned fully.

He always felt they had more time. Or needed it, at least.

Sorwin clutched a small gem in his hand, the likeness of the *indagomius*. He refocused his thoughts on sensing its twin, hoping it was still with Zak. Right now, it didn't matter how they arrived in this predicament, only that they all came out of it alive.

They were close already. Sorwin felt the *indagomius'* magic through the gem in his hand.

"Thank Cerevita," he whispered. He dipped one of his wings, lowering his altitude to be closer to Olivia, Kaleb, Bazil, and Shira.

"We're close!" he shouted, hoping his voice carried through the air at this speed. He pointed to a clearing ahead for good measure.

Below, Sorwin spotted four figures moving through the clearing, magic flying between them. From this distance, it almost looked like a dance, though Sorwin knew it to be much deadlier.

"*Visus accipiter,*" he said. His sight shifted, magically enhanced to scan the figures.

He could identify Zak and Karazul from here, though they were not fighting one another. The one with Zak was most likely Burvenin; he and Karazul seemed to work together. The fourth figure was unknown, though he saw antlers and a darker complexion. That must be the Druid the *indagomius* found.

Sorwin released his sight spell and descended, the two wyverns following close behind. They snapped at the air, the battle below exciting their predatory instincts. Sorwin and the wyverns landed a few dozen yards behind Zak and the others.

Sorwin jogged over to help Olivia, Kaleb, Bazil, and Shira dismount. As his companions slid down the sides of the beasts, they slowly backed away, making soft and light crying sounds.

Was that fear? These beasts were born for battle; they reveled in it. This didn't make any sense.

Sorwin noticed the wyverns' eyes were locked on Zak. Were they afraid of him?

Now that they were closer, Sorwin saw something had happened to Zak. What was on him? It was green, and it was on his arms and legs.

"Oh no," he said, realizing what was happening to his young apprentice.

"What is that?" Shira asked, noticing the green on Zak as well.

"Three Fires, Zakolor, what have you done?" Olivia said, her eyes flashing with guilt.

"No time to explain," Sorwin said. He had already evaluated the situation and made a plan during their descent.

"I'll need three of you to help the Druid with Karazul. Kaleb, you're the only one with a hope of getting in close."

Kaleb nodded. "I've heard of him and his skill with blades. I'll keep my guard up."

"Please do. All we need is to contain or slow him down for a short while. Olivia and Shira, support Kaleb with whatever you can. The assassin is incredibly fast, and you've already heard of his magic-negating abilities."

Olivia and Shira nodded, seeming to understand their roles.

"Bazil, see to Zak. The transformation looks more advanced than last time. Focus on slowing it down."

"I have a few ideas," Bazil said with some level of confidence.

"What about you?" Olivia asked Sorwin.

Sorwin clenched his jaw. "I'll deal with Burvenin. We have unfinished business."

Zak swiped furiously at Burvenin with his claws, no longer needing his staff. His speed had increased several times over. He should have been in awe at his newfound abilities, but all he felt was rage and desperation. Rage focused on Burvenin for all the pain he had caused Kal, his family, and Zak. And desperation to recover his friend, to prove that Burvenin was lying. It was impossible to think Kal had turned to the Consortium's side.

Even with Zak's new physical advantage, Burvenin kept up. The seasoned mage clutched a sword with two hands, deftly weaving it to his defense against each strike.

With his new sight, Zak saw a light silver glow around Burvenin's arms and sword. Was he enhancing his own speed somehow?

Before he could figure it out, a large stream of air rushed between the pair. Zak felt the force hit his chest, lifting him from the ground to push him back, putting a dozen yards between him and Burvenin.

Zak's head whirled around to see Sorwin trot to his side. His magus' eyes were wide, and his face set in uncharacteristic seriousness. Bazil trailed behind him with a similar expression and slowed a bit as he neared Zak.

"This is…" Bazil started, having difficulty analyzing Zak's physique as his eyes drifted across his arms, legs, and back to his face.

"I know what I'm doing," Zak said. He bristled under the silent judgment of Sorwin and Bazil's eyes.

They wouldn't understand, said the voice.

It was right. They *wouldn't* understand how this felt, how alive he was. How much he needed to do this for Kal, for himself.

Sorwin uttered a few words under his breath, and instantly a score of figures emerged from the earth. Their hands formed first, pulling themselves out of the ground as they manifested. As each creature found its footing, it lumbered toward Burvenin.

"The golems won't buy us much time," Sorwin said. "Let Bazil take a look at you. I'll handle Burvenin while you head for the forest."

"No!" Zak shouted. He was losing control of the situation. "I almost had him. Let me do this!"

"We don't have time, Zak! You're the one they want, you and the Druid. We need to get you out of here *now*." Sorwin emphasized the last word, but Zak didn't care.

Sorwin tried a different tactic.

"Look, all we can do is slow Karazul down. We

haven't figured out how to counter his abilities yet. Our friends—Olivia—are doing everything they can to ensure *you* are safe. If you won't leave for yourself, at least do it for them." Sorwin gestured behind him to a group of people.

Zak saw the battle between Karazul, Terasi, Olivia, and two people he didn't recognize: a man with dark hair wielding a sword and dagger and a woman with dark red hair.

Even battling Karazul four against one, Zak could tell the odds were even at best. Terasi and the dark-haired man did everything they could to keep up with Karazul's blades while Olivia and the red-haired woman lobbed spells and supported with defensive magic.

Karazul looked in his element; he countered every attack and nullified every spell. He even launched a counterattack, tripping Terasi to crash into the dark-haired man.

Zak gritted his teeth. He knew they couldn't hold long against the terrifying skills of Karazul.

You don't need long, though, do you? the voice asked.

"Let's go, Zakolor. Now is our chance," Bazil pleaded.

Zak glanced back at Burvenin. The mage had felled almost all the golems. He had only three left before his focus returned to Zak, Sorwin, and Bazil.

"You're right, now *is* our chance," Zak said.

He shoved Sorwin and Bazil in their chests, carefully avoiding hitting either of them with his claws. At this close range, and with his speed, both were caught unawares and flew back several feet.

He didn't wait to see them land. Zak turned and took off toward Burvenin, rage fueling him to incredible speeds. He could get to his enemy just before he finished with the last golem, catching him by surprise.

A flicker of movement ahead forced Zak to skid to a stop. The air shimmered and moved in front of him. What was that?

A sound like a thunderclap erupted across the clearing as the air *opened*, almost like a door, except it was violent, ripping itself into existence. It was blue and twisted, like nothing Zak had ever seen before. After a few moments, two figures emerged from the field of energy.

It was a woman he didn't recognize, and standing next to her was Kal.

His Kal.

Zak's heart stopped. He was happy to see his friend but immediately knew something was wrong. Kal looked so different. His face, ordinarily relaxed, was taught with focus.

Burvenin was right about Kal coming here. Could he be right about everything else?

"Kal!" Zak shouted. The twisting blue door behind them hung open, waiting to be closed.

Zak had no words, yet also all the words to share with his friend. Where should he start? He took a few steps toward him when Kal lifted a hand and shot a burst of deep blue fire at him.

Zak didn't have time to counter or dodge. He raised his hands in reflex to block the flames, closing his eyes and bracing for the inevitable pain.

He felt the fire hit, felt the impact on his claws and scaled arms, but that was it. No burning. Zak opened his eyes and looked over his arms. They were singed, covered in soot, and lightly smoking from the flames, but he felt no heat nor burns.

Was he immune to fire? What was happening to him?

"Kal, why did you..." Zak stammered, confusion swirling through his thoughts. "It's me, Kal! What have they done to you?" *Nothing makes any sense.*

"That's a rather rude assumption, *Nacusti*," the woman said. She had dark eyes and dark purple hair and almost glowed in the blue light from the door behind her.

There was an incredible aura of power emanating from her. He only felt something close to this with Sorwin and Tansil; their respective magics always filled a room.

But this woman. Her presence was stifling.

"He's here of his own free will, I'll have you know," she continued. A fiendish smile cracked her face. "At least you were helpful and brought me my Druid." Her eyes darted to the right, where Terasi and the others battled Karazul.

Zak tried to ignore her and focus on his friend. "Kal, please, what's happening? Come home, back to Densba. We can—"

More dark blue flames shot toward Zak. This time, he put up a small emerald shield to deflect the spell. His eyes widened in disbelief. Why was his friend attacking him?

Sorwin appeared at Zak's side, putting his hands on his shoulders and pulling him back a few steps. "That isn't the friend you lost, Zakolor. He's someone else now," Sorwin said solemnly.

Zak looked up at Sorwin, still in shock. While the mage talked about Kal, Zak saw his eyes locked on the woman.

"You're Renna, aren't you?" Sorwin asked the woman.

"Sorwin Darlangson," she replied, her twisted smile growing a little wider. "I'm flattered you've heard of me. The pleasure is mine." Renna gave a small curtsy, her blue and black robes rippling as she moved.

"Renna? You mean..." Zak started.

"Zandorn's daughter," Sorwin finished.

It made sense why Zak felt so much power from her. Zandorn was one of the most powerful mages in Valecium since Zak's ancestor, Adrastus, sealed the gods away in the Guardian War. There was no telling how powerful his daughter could be.

Powerful enough to twist Kal's mind, perhaps. It was the only thing that made sense.

Burvenin walked to stand next to Renna, brushing dirt off his sleeves from the last golem he destroyed.

"Clever trick, I'll give you that one, Sorwin. Haven't seen golems like that in a few decades," Burvenin said. He almost sounded amused.

Sorwin didn't seem to be listening as he turned to Zak, gently but firmly using his hands to square Zak's shoulders to face him. As he did, everything around Zak changed. The color seemed to fade from the world, and movement slowed to a near standstill.

"Do you trust me, Zakolor?" he asked.

Zak's head felt muddy. Waves of emotion and confusion hit him, and he struggled to form coherent thoughts.

"I...where..." he stammered.

"This is important," Sorwin said, genuine care and concern in his eyes. "Do you trust me?" he repeated.

"Yes," Zak said, this time without hesitation. It was the truth.

"I've brought us to the astral plane so we could speak. I can do the same with Kal, but only for a few moments. That's all the time you'll have to either convince him to come with us or let him go. Do you understand?"

Zak nodded. The chance to speak with Kal gave him clarity and direction. This was what he had been waiting for, working toward since the moment he left Densba.

"How will you—" Zak began to ask.

"Leave the 'how' to me," Sorwin said with a smile. Zak wondered if it was the first time the mage resisted answering a question. "Be ready in case Kal isn't receptive. You may need to defend yourself again."

"I'll be fine. I'm not leaving without him," Zak stated resolutely.

Sorwin nodded and jogged toward where Renna, Kal, and Burvenin stood on the physical plane. "I hope you're right. Kal will be here in a few seconds. I'll distract Burvenin and Renna for as long as I can." With that, Zak's magus disappeared in a cloud of smoke.

CHAPTER 23
VOICES

Sorwin appeared directly behind Kal on the physical plane. His arms and legs tensed, his entire body prepared to spring into action. All he had to do was make physical contact with Kal, but he had mere seconds to get this next part right.

It felt like everything was happening in half time. He reached forward with his left hand and shoved Kal forward. As Kal stumbled, he disappeared in a cloud of smoke, phasing to the astral plane.

As soon as Sorwin reappeared, Burvenin had launched a flurry of fireballs in his direction. Sorwin had no time for a shield, he was wide open having stretched to reach Kal.

He had no choice, he had to use a new spell he was working on. It wasn't quite ready, still experimental, not perfected, and therefore high-risk, but it was better than facing a direct hit with Burvenin's attack.

Sorwin disappeared in a flash of blue light, which crackled around his body like lightning. He reappeared in less than an instant a dozen yards in front of where he had been standing, close to the forest's tree line.

He let out a sigh of relief, happy his teleportation spell had worked. Burvenin's fireballs crashed harmlessly into the ground where he had been standing a moment before, scorching and burning the grass, and mushrooming a cloud of dirt into the air.

Renna didn't move throughout the exchange, but Sorwin knew her eyes tracked him diligently.

"Seems you're further along than I thought," Renna said, still unmoving with her arms crossed. "I didn't think the League had figured out teleportation."

"We're certainly not as advanced as you," Sorwin said with a nod to the portal still hanging behind Renna. The twisting and crackling blue light was not dissimilar to his spell. "But we're on our way. I wouldn't turn down any hints, though. How did you manage to open a portal here without an anchor?" Sorwin couldn't help himself. Even in the middle of a battle, his curiosity bested him.

"Who said I didn't have one?" Renna retorted casually. Her eyes flicked to Burvenin briefly, but it was long enough for Sorwin to see and understand.

"Of course!" he said. He smiled as he connected several thoughts and theories to form a new idea. "A *living* anchor, how genius!"

"You really are a bright mage; my father was right," Renna said. She nodded to Burvenin. "He's your quarry, isn't he? We're not here to discuss magical theory. End him, Burvenin, before I do it for you."

"It would be my pleasure," Burvenin grunted, silver

flames erupting in his hands and crawling up his arms.

Sorwin's smile faded, knowing he had to focus. According to Tansil, Burvenin was among the most powerful fire mages in the last three centuries, making his element choice rather obvious.

A stream of water flowed from Sorwin's right hand, creating a ring that circled him as his body tensed again. He had faced Burvenin before, but this time was different. This time, his focus was squarely on Sorwin and not on kidnapping anyone. This time, he knew, it was a battle to the death.

Zak breathed heavily, the excitement of fighting Burvenin and seeing his friend again racing through his lungs and veins. The toll of the magic he wielded was also catching up, wreaking havoc on his body.

He looked down at his hands and feet, or what used to be his hands and feet. They looked like they belonged to a giant lizard now, not a young mage. What was happening?

This is what you wanted, said the voice. *Power dwells within you, Parignis. This is what it looks like.*

"I..." Zak stammered. "I don't know...wait. *Parignis?* That's what Terasi called me. How did you—"

Before he could finish his question, a cloud of smoke appeared a few yards away. As it dissipated, Kal stumbled forward.

Zak could see his eyes were wide, perhaps with panic or confusion. He nervously whipped around, evaluating his surroundings before his gaze landed on Zak.

"You," Kal said. "What have you done? What has *he* done?" His teeth gritted, barely parting as he spoke. Zak could almost feel his friend's anger and confusion through his words.

"Kal, we don't have much time. I'm so sorry for everything. You never should have been taken. This is all my fault—"

Kal interrupted his apology by thrusting a hand forward.

Zak flinched, pulling his arms up to cover his face, expecting another stream of fire. He waited for the impact, but nothing came.

Zak peeked between his arms to see Kal looking just as confused, his brow furrowing and his teeth now fully visible through his snarl.

"Where are we?!" Kal shouted, demanding an answer more than asking a question.

"We're in the astral plane. Magic must work differently here," Zak surmised. Sorwin didn't have time to explain, but he was sure he would get the entire lesson if they both survived the day.

Kal paced around the spot he had arrived in the astral plane, apparently looking for a way out. His movements were quick and rigid, and his expression never softened, staying taut with anger.

This was not his friend; Sorwin was right. This was not the bright, sensitive boy who cared for Zak and watched out for him their entire childhood. This wasn't him, but Zak was determined to find him.

His claws clacked against his scales as his fists closed and opened, his nerves jittering beneath his scales.

"Kal, I can't imagine what you've been through with the Consortium. I'm sorry you're wrapped up in this mess because of me. If you come with me, with us, I'm sure Sorwin can help you."

"Help me what?" Kal yelled. He turned and took several steps toward Zak, his eyes wild. "What is it, exactly, that you think *I* need help with?"

"I didn't mean—" Zak started. The tips of his ears burned.

"You don't 'mean' a lot of things, yet here we are!" Kal threw his arms open to the sides to emphasize his point. "What were you hoping would happen here, Zak? That we'd have a little reunion and everything would be fine?"

"No, I don't know, I thought—"

"No, you didn't think, Zak! You never have! That's why I *always* had to look out for you." Kal took a few more steps forward, his focus settling on Zak.

As Kal moved closer, his presence was stronger, more stifling, similar to Renna. What had they done to change him so much in such a short amount of time?

His friend was now an arm's length away.

"Why did they bring you here, Kal?" Zak asked. Tears welled at the corners of his eyes, threatening to spill over and down his cheeks.

For the first time since seeing him, Kal smiled. It wasn't *his* smile, though. It was wicked and twisted.

"For you, of course. Once we knew you were here, I knew

I had to come get you."

Kal thrust his hands forward, closing a tight grip around Zak's throat.

Zak's airflow stopped, forcing a gasp to escape as his body tried to keep breathing. At the same time, he felt Kal's magic and presence in his mind as his friend glowed a dark blue.

"What are you—" Zak winced, barely able to speak through Kal's crushing grip.

"This will be much easier if you come willingly," Kal said. The ferocity on his face intensified, and so did the magic surrounding him. He looked more like a wild animal than a person.

Zak felt weak. It was the lack of air, but there was something else too. His magic was slipping away—no, not slipping, *draining*. It was similar to how it felt after he used a lot of magic, like it was all gone.

Break the connection! said the voice. *He's stealing your power!*

Zak glanced at his hands, clutching Kal's arms. His claws had punctured Kal's skin as tiny dots of blood pooled, but his friend didn't seem to notice in his crazed state. But now his claws began to fade, and his human fingers reappeared as the green scales receded up his arms.

Kal's mind probed his own, trying to find a way in. He didn't know how, but he was confident Kal was attempting to control his thoughts. It was like he could feel Kal's stream of consciousness as he entered Zak's. He felt something else, too, or *someone* else.

It was Renna.

Panic surged through him. He didn't know her, but the feeling he had from her was unmistakable. She was in Kal's mind, her thoughts and feelings intertwined with his, wrapping around him in a shroud. Was this why he was so different? Was Renna controlling him in some way?

He had to do something now. He needed to save Kal.

The magic wasn't completely gone from his arms; a few scattered scales remained, and so did his heightened strength. He pulled hard on Kal's arms, wresting the grip from his throat.

Kal's eyes widened in confusion. Zak pushed harder, throwing his friend off and forcing him to stumble back a few steps, breaking their contact. Zak immediately felt the draining of his magic stop. It seemed it was dependent on physical contact.

Before he could do anything, there was a pulling sensation in his chest. A cloud of smoke rolled around his body. As it faded, color returned to his surroundings. Sorwin's spell had worn off; he was back on the physical plane.

Kal was a few steps away, brought back at the same time. His magic still shrouded him in a dark blue glow, but now a bright emerald hue surrounded his hands.

"Is that my magic?" Zak wondered aloud. That means...

"Zak!" He looked up in time to see Olivia sprinting toward him. Her auburn hair flew wild behind her, and her red and silver uniform was covered in dirt and other residue. She slowed as she neared him, catching her breath.

"Are you okay?" he asked, grasping her shoulder. It felt forward, but it also felt right in the moment.

Olivia didn't seem to notice. "I'm fine. Bazil took my place against Karazul." She gestured behind her. A glance showed Zak the battle with the dangerous assassin continued. From here, it looked nearly even still; Karazul managed to hold his ground against Terasi, Bazil, and the man and woman Zak didn't know. His breath caught in awe of Karazul, but he didn't have time to focus on him. He needed to save his friend.

Zak looked back at Kal, who was having some kind of struggle. He kept staring at his hands, shaking his head, and blinking as if a battle waged in his mind. Zak didn't know how much more time he had before Kal regained his composure.

"I need your help." Zak shifted his attention back to Olivia. "I think I know how to save Kal, but I can't do it alone. I need you to restrain him somehow."

"I was going to help Sorwin, Bazil said—" Olivia started.

"Please." Zak's tone was more desperate than he would have liked. "Please," he tried again. "This might be my only chance."

Olivia's face tightened, and her mouth hardened into a straight line. Her eyes darted from Sorwin to himself.

Zak took a moment to look at his magus' battle. Sorwin and Burvenin seemed evenly matched. It was difficult to track the speed at which they moved and the complexity of the spells they wove. Explosions of fire and water erupted at what seemed like random intervals, though Zak knew it was anything but random.

Theirs was a magical duel the likes of which Zak had never witnessed.

Olivia let out a sigh that sounded frustrated. "Bazil seemed to think I could help Sorwin, but I might just get in his way. He and Burvenin are both monsters."

She took a moment to settle her eyes on Zak, seeming to evaluate him before doing the same to Kal. "Fine, what do you need?"

Zak nodded his thanks and almost smiled momentarily, though he was too focused to let his emotions out of check now.

"Stop him from moving. If I can make physical contact with him, I think I can help him.""I have just the spell," Olivia said, her usual confidence finding its way into her voice again. "Try not to use too much fire, whatever you do," she instructed.

"Hopefully, I won't need to." Zak faced Kal. "Whenever you're ready."

Zak couldn't see Olivia behind him, but he felt the surge of her magic as she prepared her spell and released it.

"*Sylvaligo*," she said, crouching to the ground and thrusting her hands into the earth.

The ground rippled with movement, pushing up in some areas as it shot toward Kal. Wooden branches burst through the ground at his feet, wrapping around Kal's ankles and moving up his legs. More branches reached for his wrists and waist, continuing to crawl around him as they lifted him just a few inches off the ground.

As his friend hung there, suspended and writhing, he reminded Zak of a twisted version of a scarecrow from the farms in his hometown.

Kal was only a few steps away, so reaching his friend took only a moment. He hesitated, his hands hovering next to his friend's torso.

"What are you doing?" Kal grunted. He snapped out of whatever trance he had been in; his eyes were wild again, but Zak could see there was still a struggle in his mind.

"I'm learning from you," Zak replied.

He placed his hands gently but firmly on Kal's shoulders. Immediately, the draining sensation returned, and this time, he recognized his magic moving into Kal. The dark blue shroud flared to life around Kal, matching the emerald green one that had grown around Zak. Maintaining the connection was exhausting and challenging, but he had to.

Zak felt Kal's thoughts and consciousness again. He wanted to try something.

Kal? Can you hear me? He projected the thought toward Kal's mind.

Zak? Kal sounded distant, his voice almost echoing. *What's happening?*

I don't know, Zak answered honestly. *I'm following a hunch. Thinking, like you said I should. But it's helping. I feel Renna's hold on you weakening.*

And it was. Zak could almost see the shroud in Kal's thoughts and feelings begin to evaporate, little pieces breaking off and dissolving like embers in a fire.

"NO!" Zak heard a woman shout. At some point, he had closed his eyes, and opening them now, he saw Renna staring at Zak and Kal. Her earlier composure melted away and was replaced with a familiar ferocity. It looked and felt the same as

Kal's had earlier.

She can feel what you're doing, Kal said. *We don't have much time. You have to let me go. She won't kill you since you're the* Nacusti, *but she'll kill everyone else here.*

No! I can't! Not when we're so close.

You're losing your strength. You should listen to what he wants and let him go, the voice said.

Who is that? Kal asked.

You can hear it, too? Zak was almost happy for a moment. *Three Fires, at least I'm not insane.*

That's still up for debate, given our current situation, Kal chided, almost playfully. For the briefest of moments, Zak felt he had his friend back, and a slight smirk broke the tension on his face.

I'm not letting you go, Zak told the voice as much as Kal.

Get ready, then, the voice said. *This will hurt.*

CHAPTER 24

CONSEQUENCES

"Enough!" Renna yelled.

Zak didn't think it was possible, but Renna's presence grew even more prominent in his mind. Her magic swelled as she raised her arm to the side, keeping her eyes on Zak and Kal as crimson flames erupted from her outstretched palm toward the forest.

The fiery torrent was enormous. It was at least twice as tall as Renna, devastating all the grass, trees, and earth it touched. While the magic looked like fire, it was more than that. It devoured everything in its path. Thousands of trees disintegrated in an instant. When the flames cleared, there was nothing left but a dark, burned trench in the ground, stretching into the distance beyond Zak's sight.

"Agh!" Zak heard the cry of pain and then saw Terasi fall to one knee. His hand clutched his chest like the fire had struck *him*.

It had, in a way, Zak quickly reasoned. What little Sorwin shared about Druids was that their power was connected to nature, to the forests they tended.

That was her intent, Zak thought. *To weaken Terasi.*

"Now, Karazul. Stop playing and retrieve Kalbick. My father is expecting us," Renna instructed.

Karazul nodded and turned toward Zak and Kal, beginning a steady march toward them.

The dark-haired man jumped before Karazul, swinging his sword and dagger at the dangerous man.

Karazul swatted the attacks aside and launched a flurry of strikes in return, overwhelming his opponent with speed. The assassin deftly wove his blades through the air, the metal moving like extensions of his arms. Karazul snuck a blade inside the man's left guard, flinging his arm out wide before reversing his blade, slashing diagonally down his torso.

The sword was so sharp and the cut so clean it took a moment for the stream of red to emerge from the man's skin, following the same path as the blade. His eyes widened, his senses seemingly catching up with the wound. He gasped and crumpled to the ground, his sword and dagger clanging harmlessly to the earth beside him.

"Kaleb!" Olivia yelled.

Zak clenched his jaw. He didn't know Kaleb, only by name from his brief time in Tor'alan. He was rumored to be one of the best swordsmen in the League's army, yet Karazul managed him like a child with a toy sword. Kaleb came here to save Zak; he risked his life for the *Nacusti*. Zak was tired of others getting hurt for his sake.

Bazil was on the ground nearby and crawled toward Kaleb, presumably to try to heal him.

Karazul resumed his march toward Zak and Kal. Zak's chest tightened and his stomach dropped as the deadly man approached.

What could he do? He felt how close he was to saving Kal, to releasing him from Renna's hold. But he had to maintain contact to do so. His magic continued to drain steadily too. He couldn't move, couldn't cast a spell. What could he do?

There was a flutter of movement to his right, and the red-haired woman attacked Karazul this time. She launched a stream of purple fire at the assassin. Karazul raised a hand, nullifying the magic before it ever reached him.

She maintained the fire, reaching for something in a pocket with her other hand. She pulled out a small blue orb, no bigger than the palm of her hand, with bright colors swirling under its glassy surface.

"I have this one," Renna said to Karazul. "We don't need any demons helping these insects."

Crimson flames appeared behind the woman, wrapping swiftly around her wrists and waist. She let out a yelp as the flames buckled her knees and dragged her to the ground, pinning her in place.

"She bound...my magic," the woman managed to say loud enough for Zak to hear.

"Shira—hold on!" Bazil yelled.

Another sacrifice for the Nacusti. *How many do you require?* the voice asked in Zak's head. It almost sounded like it was enjoying the spectacle.

Shut up!

But it was right. Kaleb and Shira were among a growing

list of people who risked everything to save him. Anger flared inside him, almost outweighing the fear he felt seeing Karazul march toward him and Kal. The assassin was less than a dozen steps away now.

Before Zak could think or do anything, Olivia stepped in Karazul's path, and the assassin gave her a crooked smile.

"You know, I enjoyed our dance today. I can't remember the last time I was pushed this far," Karazul said. "I'd prefer to continue, but duty calls, as you heard." He gestured behind him toward Renna with a lazy wave of one of his blades.

"Hurry up and finish what you started," Olivia told Zak, ignoring Karazul's taunting. "I'll buy you what time I can."

Zak grunted his thanks and pushed more magic into Kal, feeling Renna's hold weakening further, slow but consistent. He kept his eyes on Olivia. He couldn't let another person sacrifice themselves for him. Especially not her.

Olivia wasted no time. Her arms moved in a blur as spells strung from her lips.

The earth around Karazul's feet sharpened into spikes and flung themselves at the man. He danced and dodged a few paces back, arcing his blades to cut the spikes that came too close.

Olivia was already on to her next spell. The same wooden binding spell she used on Kal burst through the ground behind Karazul, twisting and crawling up his arms and legs. The branches quickly wrenched his arms out wide.

Karazul's smile widened as he dropped his swords and grabbed onto the branches. Zak wasn't sure what happened, whether Karazul absorbed or nullified the magic, but after a few moments, he snapped the branches with a twist of his wrist as if they were nothing more than dry twigs.

Just as Karazul freed himself, Olivia sent a torrent of water flying from her left hand. Karazul blocked the magic with his hand and ran toward Olivia, cutting through the stream of water as he did.

Olivia drew the sword at her hip, dropping the water magic as Karazul neared. She swung down hard with her sword.

Karazul caught Olivia's wrist at the top of her swing with his free hand, twisted to change the blade's direction, then pushed to finish the arc.

Zak saw the blade swing in a silver flash and suddenly appear halfway through Olivia's side, her blood dotting the metal. She coughed once as she slowly bent to her knees, her hands still clutching the hilt of the blade sticking through her.

"Olivia!" Zak yelled, his voice cracking. This was all his fault, his doing. He was responsible for her injuries, maybe for her death.

Karazul let go of the blade as Olivia lowered to the ground, his eyes on Zak, reveling in his terror.

Except Zak felt no terror, not now. All he felt was rage and anger. It boiled within him throughout this entire battle.

Throughout his entire journey to Tor'alan.

Ever since Kal was taken instead of him.

Zak looked into Karazul's eyes. His hatred for the man and all his rage was coming out now.

It's time, the voice said. *Let it out.*

Zak yelled or screamed. He didn't know and didn't care.

His lungs and throat blazed with pain as the air ignited in emerald fire around him. He didn't need to reach for his magic. It was all right there at his fingertips.

He felt an explosion of magic as the fire expanded. It grew fast, pushing out in every direction from where he stood.

The fire reached Olivia first and Karazul immediately after. The assassin put an arm in front of him, supposedly to nullify the magic, but nothing happened. The fire kept pushing.

Karazul's eyes widened as the wall of emerald fire pushed him back. It singed his palm and fingers before he fell and rolled backward to safety.

The fire kept moving. It was a dome shape, expanding further and further with Zak at the center. Next, the fire reached the woman Renna had attacked—Shira. Zak's emerald flames burned through Renna's crimson ones, releasing her and leaving her unharmed.

Zak barely felt anything anymore. His mind was nearly blank, given over to emotion and action. He retained a sliver of control, enough to direct the spell. He felt another presence, too. Like someone else was in his mind.

He looked down. His claws had returned, along with the green scales on his arms. They reached further this time, disappearing under his shirt. He felt the fabric on his back tear and a sharp pain pierce his shoulders. A woosh of air blew past his face. He craned his neck to see two wings sprouting from his back.

It felt like his whole body was on fire, his transformation going further than ever before.

I warned you this would hurt, the voice said.

It doesn't matter, Zak answered. *We need to keep going.* He didn't know what he was or what was happening, but he knew he was gaining power from it, so he pushed harder.

The fire shield reached Bazil and Kaleb next, the priest struggling with his own injuries as he healed the swordsman on the ground in front of him.

With a thought, Zak reached Bazil with his magic and levitated the priest, floating him toward Olivia.

"Zak!" Bazil shouted in midair. "What's happening?" The priest looked bewildered as he flew through the air.

"Heal her! There's no time!" Zak yelled to Bazil. The priest's eyes darted from Olivia to Zak several times before Zak dropped him on the ground next to Olivia.

The giant dome of fire slowed, seeming to reach its limit. It was at least a few dozen yards in diameter now. Zak reached out with his magic to gently lift and pull Kaleb and Shira closer to Bazil, hoping he could heal them after he saved Olivia. Their bodies flew limply through the air, but he could feel they were both still alive.

Straight ahead, Karazul backed up with every inch the shield took. The assassin looked confused as he tried to nullify the emerald flames again.

Zak felt something happen to the spell when he did. It felt similar to the draining effect Kal's magic had on him. But Karazul's drain was too weak to stop him. His rage deepened his vast reserves, and for every piece of the spell Karazul drained, Zak replaced it tenfold.

He knew the shield couldn't expand further, but that was

okay. Zak looked around and saw almost everyone from the League was inside now. To his left, he heard Sorwin's battle continued. Terasi crouched on the ground to his right, still wounded from the loss of so much of his forest.

Zak started to reach out with his magic to bring Terasi under the shield. Before he could, crimson flames blazed around the Druid. They looked similar to the ones that had attacked Shira earlier, except this time, they wrapped around Terasi in a coil from head to toe, immobilizing him entirely. Rather than pinning him to the ground, the flames levitated the druid, floating him beside Renna.

"This prize is coming with me, at the very least," Renna shouted above the blaze of Zak's flames.

Zak gritted his teeth. He was protecting Kaleb, Shira, and Bazil. The priest was working on Olivia now, his hands glowing a bright turquoise color as they moved fast but delicately around her wound.

He still had one hand on Kal, the constant drain of his magic funneling into his friend. Kal's eyes were closed, and he was near motionless, save for his shallow breathing. How much longer would this take? How long could he hold the connection, transformation, and shield spell?

Sorwin breathed heavily, the strain of his magic catching up. His clothes were tattered, and his body beneath was dotted with minor burns where Burvenin's fire connected.

His opponent was in a similar form. His muscled frame

heaved with exhaustion and numerous cuts dripped small streams of blood down his arms and torso. Sorwin would have marveled at how closely matched their powers were in any other scenario, but now was not that time. Not when the lives of so many depended on him.

With that thought, he glanced to his right, seeing Zak's emerald shield expand. His companions seemed safe for the moment, but how long could Zak hold the spell? Sorwin didn't want to find out; he needed to finish this battle fast to protect them.

Sorwin's eyes flashed back to Burvenin. Their struggle had told him much so far. Burvenin's attacks were simple and direct but packed with so much power that any direct hit could be enough to finish Sorwin, or at least incapacitate him. He had survived by dodging and deflecting, though the minor burns on his body proved not every spell was stoppable. Even with proper shields, Burvenin's spells pushed through his defenses a few times.

"I didn't want to do this," Sorwin started. "I wanted to defeat you with my own power, but time is not my ally now." As he spoke, he reached into the pocket in his robe and pulled out a small leather purse. His fingers released the strings and gently pulled out a palm-sized jewel with an impossible number of colors streaking through it.

"Finally seeing you're outmatched, are you?" Burvenin smirked, straightening his stance as he caught his breath. His eyes narrowed as he peered toward Sorwin's hands. "What's this? Another trick?"

Sorwin wasn't listening. He looked down as he muttered

a spell, the jewel hovering between his hands. It began rotating, slow at first and then increasing in speed until it appeared to be a solid sphere.

The air around Sorwin hummed with energy and took on an orange tint that matched his magic. When he finished his spell and looked up, his vision had changed, heightened somehow, and green around the edges. He saw the energy of all living things in the field flowing, from a single blade of grass to the carrion birds circling overhead, waiting for a meal to present itself. Sorwin knew from his experience with the stone that his eyes shone pure green now, filled with magical energy.

Burvenin must have sensed the change in Sorwin's magic as he took a hesitant half-step backward. "Don't threaten me unless you plan to follow through," he growled through gritted teeth. He was like a cornered animal, raising his hackles at the prospect of death.

"Leave this place," Sorwin heard his voice say. It echoed like there were several voices behind his own. His mind and body burned with energy. Channeling this power was too much for him to sustain for any length of time, but he hoped it was enough to save Zak and his companions in their time of need.

Burvenin didn't respond with words. He launched a flurry of silver fireballs toward Sorwin.

A wall of water erupted, catching the fireballs as they hissed harmlessly into steam. With a twitch of his hand, Sorwin turned the water wall into a wave as it pushed itself forward toward Burvenin.

With his heightened sight, Sorwin could see through the mass of water that Burvenin attempted to split the flood, clasping his hands in a spear shape before him. It worked for a few moments, but the sheer volume of water seemed unending. Sorwin moved a finger, directing the water that passed Burvenin to circle back around.

The water swallowed Burvenin from behind, the shock on his face plain as it crashed into him from all directions. Sorwin saw his body tumble through the water as he directed random currents to keep his dangerous opponent trapped. There was so much water it looked like a large pond had lost its earthen banks, standing on its own more than a dozen feet tall.

Sweat matted Sorwin's shirt to his back, and he knew he was reaching his limit. In one last effort, he clapped his hands in front of him and pushed with all the magical force he could muster, causing the pool of water to pressurize like the darkest depths of the deepest ocean. He watched as the life energy around Burvenin flickered out like a dying candle.

Sorwin released the spell, falling to his knees and gasping for air as the toll of the grand magic set in on his body. The jewel fell to the ground next to him. The water, a moment ago so deadly, cascaded in a rush to run through the field.

Burvenin's body fell with the water, floating to the right a few yards as the liquid carried him briefly before soaking into the earth. There he remained, motionless.

Sorwin gently picked up the jewel and placed it back in the leather purse, tucking it into his robe. He struggled to his feet, panting as he stood. His face darkened with a final glance at Burvenin's still body. He knew it was the right thing to do, to protect his companions with his limited options, yet it pained him deeply to take a life.

"May you find peace with Our Lady Cerevita," he whispered, weaving the traditional life sign before turning and moving toward Zakolor.

"Sorwin!" Zak called as his magus jogged slowly toward him. Sorwin's hue was ashen, and minor scorches covered the skin visible through his ruined tunic, but his eyes appeared clear and focused.

Sorwin paused briefly at the perimeter of Zak's fire shield, hovering a hand near its edge as if testing it somehow. He took a cautious step through the barrier, emerging unscathed and moving to stand at Zak's side.

"Are you uninjured?" Sorwin asked, his expression severe but quizzical as he studied Zak's transformation and clawed hands that still grasped Kal's shoulders.

"Mostly, I think," Zak answered, gritting his teeth through the constant drain of his magic.

Zak watched as Sorwin's gaze snapped from Zak to Kal, to straight above them at the apex of the significant barrier, over to where Renna and Karazul stalked the perimeter, onto Bazil and his patients, and finally back to Kal. Zak knew the mage well enough now to understand he was evaluating their situation and how best to escape it.

"How long can you keep the shield up?" Sorwin asked.

"Not much longer, but I can't let go of Kal. He's draining my magic, and I can't explain it, but I know it's helping. I can feel his mind, and I feel him recovering from whatever they did to him."

Sorwin blinked, unmoving for a moment. "I know Kal is your priority, Zakolor. Just as you and everyone that came with me to rescue you are my priority." Sorwin took a short breath. "We need to focus on getting out of here together so we can help Kal together."

It was Zak's turn to pause and breathe. He stared at the battle-weary mage before his eyes slid to Bazil and the others. The orange afternoon sun filtered through the trees behind Bazil, silhouetting him as he still worked on Olivia's wounds.

Zak knew he was helping Kal. He could feel it in every bone in his body and with every beat of his heart. He also knew he was running out of magic and time. Eventually, his shield would give out, and it was the only thing protecting them from Karazul and Renna. If he kept this up, he would be choosing to save Kal at the cost of everyone else who came to rescue him.

"What do we do?" he asked Sorwin, feeling the weight of the choice on his shoulders.

"*Dormiligo,*" Sorwin said, pressing his hand to Kal's forehead as he did. Kal's head drooped so his chin rested on his chest, his body still suspended in the wooden bind Olivia had conjured.

"That will keep him in a deep sleep for a time. Hopefully, long enough for us to find out what you were fixing."

Zak nodded, the tension in his body easing as he looked

at his sleeping friend. Kal's consciousness slipped away the moment Sorwin used his spell, and as soon as their physical connection broke, so too did the drain on Zak's magic. He felt so close to finally saving Kal but so confused by what had happened to his friend.

Suddenly, he felt another pull on his magic. Karazul was at the edge of the barrier, testing it again with his strange ability.

"They have Terasi," Zak told Sorwin, gesturing with a clawed hand to the limp Druid hanging in midair behind Renna. As he did, the fearsome woman stepped toward Zak, stopping at the edge of the barrier, though her eyes seemed to penetrate his very being.

Simultaneously, his barrier and the portal behind Renna flickered, both shrinking momentarily and wavering in strength.

"It seems we're both at our limits," Renna called to Zak. "Next time, I won't miscalculate."

With a wave of her hand, Burvenin's corpse flew in the air toward Renna.

"Of course, her anchor is gone. The portal is closing!" Sorwin said.

Zak didn't know what an anchor was but knew the dangers of closing portals. That's how he lost Kal in the first place.

"That means—they're getting away with Terasi!" he yelled.

Renna and Karazul turned toward the portal as Terasi floated through, still wrapped in crimson flames, followed by Burvenin's hovering corpse. Without looking back, the remaining pair walked through as the portal blinked closed behind them.

Zak's chest tightened as he watched Terasi disappear. He felt something else, not quite relief, but more of a release as the dangerous group left. He dropped to his scaly knees as his barrier dissipated.

"I failed again," Zak whispered to himself.

Sorwin sighed, perhaps in relief or perhaps at his young apprentice. He crouched in front of Zak, putting both hands on his shoulders.

"Failure is a perspective and part of learning. If you're alive, you can keep learning. And besides," Sorwin continued, grunting as he stood upright. "None of this was what we intended. You did more than anyone expected."

Zak nodded, hearing the wisdom in Sorwin's words, even if he wasn't ready to admit it. Returning somewhat to his senses, his eyes widened once again.

"Olivia!" he half crawled, half ran to his friend. Bazil knelt by her side, his hands glowing in his turquoise magic.

"How is she?" Zak asked. He hesitated as he reached to touch her arm in a comforting reflex but pulled back at the sight of his clawed limbs.

Bazil's eyes didn't leave Olivia as he spoke. "It's not good," he told Zak as Sorwin walked behind them. "I can feel her spirit still, but she's fading fast."

"Why isn't the healing magic working?" Zak asked, more frantic than he meant.

"I can't perform miracles," Bazil countered sharply. "I

can only speed the healing process, not reverse fatal wounds."

Zak looked down at Olivia. She was always so strong, so forceful. Lying on the ground, she seemed so different, almost helpless. He looked up to Sorwin, feeling tears blaze down his cheeks.

"Sorwin, she's not...she can't be," he stammered. He turned back to Olivia and grabbed her hand with his green-scaled claw. She felt colder than the ocean water near his island home in winter.

The last thing he remembered was Sorwin shouting his name before everything went dark.

CHAPTER 25

IDENTITY

Zak heard the familiar rhythmic crashing of ocean waves on a shoreline. He sat up too fast, and his head spun for a moment as he looked around.

He was on a strange beach. The water and sky were dark. There was no sun or moon, nor torches or fires, yet a faint glimmer of green appeared at the crest of waves and edges of the cliffs behind him. His eyes searched for a light source but found none, as if it had shifted just out of sight when his gaze found the light. It gave the entire beach an eerie glow.

"You finally made it," a deep voice said behind him.

Zak scrambled to his feet, his heart pounding. He realized his hands and feet were back to normal, absent of scales and claws. A glance over his shoulder found there were no wings, either.

"Who are you?" Zak asked. The green glow illuminated the beach enough he would have seen someone standing within a few dozen paces.

"I'm hurt you don't recognize my voice," it replied.

"You!" Zak said. "You're the voice I've been hearing."

"Indeed. You're bright for a *Nacusti*."

Zak scowled at the title, hearing the voice's disdain in its tone. As Zak continued searching for the source of the voice, he saw a dark crevice along the cliffside that looked like a cave opening.

"So you've met other *Nacusti*, then?" He took a few wary steps forward to test his theory.

"All of them," the voice said flatly.

That gave Zak pause. "All—how is that possible? You'd have to be as old as Tansil."

A cold laugh came from the voice, sending a shiver down Zak's spine. He heard it echo off the walls of what he knew now to be a cave. He knew where the voice came from but couldn't see its owner.

"You dare compare me to that sapling? I retract my previous statement. Perhaps you are as dim as the rest of your kind."

Zak heard movement from inside the cave. It sounded like a rock slide he had witnessed years ago, boulders crashing down the side of a mountain. The very earth he stood on shook with vibrations. Whatever was in there was enormous and was coming out.

He took a few cautious steps backward, feeling the muscles along his legs and arms tense. He didn't know if he was preparing to run or fight.

Zak nearly fell as the creature emerged. A large, green-scaled head snaked out from the cave and into the eerie green light of the beach. Its long snout held countless arched teeth longer than Zak's torso. Golden eyes shone bright in stark contrast to their surroundings.

The beach shook with each step the creature took, and soon Zak saw why. A long, serpentine neck connected its head to a massive, four-legged body. Its muscles rippled across its chest and legs as it sauntered from the cave. Two scaly wings folded along its back, and a long tail drifted lazily through the air behind the beast.

"Y-you're—" Zak stammered.

"Jolsu, the Sky Emerald and Guardian of mankind," the beast answered.

Zak swallowed hard and took in the enormous figure in front of him.

"You're the Guardian, the dragon that fused with Adrastus," Zak said, putting his thoughts together as he spoke.

Jolsu said nothing, his golden eyes staring down at Zak as his tail flicked lazily from side to side.

"Where are we? How is this possible?"

"You really are a disappointment," Jolsu scoffed. "Look around. Where do you *think* we are?"

Zak managed to temporarily tear his gaze away from the imposing dragon to reevaluate his surroundings. The strange green light was odd, but the beach itself felt familiar. He had been here before.

"This is Carshandyn!" he said. Recognizing his home island fueled his excitement. "I used to come here with Kal when we were little, and we played in that very cave."

Jolsu's head nodded once. "It is Carshandyn, yet not at all," he countered.

Zak's excitement left him as fast as it came. His smile

faded as he considered the dragon's words.

Of course, they couldn't *actually* be on Carshandyn, he reasoned.

"The last thing I remember was the battle with Renna and Karazul and finally saving Kal. And then…" his thoughts felt muddy. For a few moments, only the gentle waves could be heard repeatedly pushing into the shore before sliding back into the ocean.

"We're in my head," Zak said at last, calmly returning his gaze to Jolsu.

"Perhaps there is hope for you yet," the dragon said. The earth shook again as Jolsu settled to a lying position, his front legs extending forward to display his long, dangerous claws.

"Why haven't we spoken like this before?" Zak asked. "It was always whispers. I thought I was mad when I first started hearing you."

"Yes, that was good fun," the edges of Jolsu's mouth twisted into a smile, showing his long teeth.

"You're enjoying this?" Zak pressed. He felt a twinge of anger and confusion. "I don't understand. You gave me your power earlier. You helped me stay alive. You must have done that for a reason. If you're here inside me, you must need me alive?"

Jolsu's tail flicked behind him, faster this time. "Alive, yes. Sane? Not entirely. You are the last *Nacusti* in your line, meaning I only need you to make little *Nacustis*, and then you're no longer useful. But you mistake my temporary need for you to live with a desire to help. I will help you only enough to keep you alive, and I might as well be entertained while I do it."

"Does that mean you're alive?" Zak asked, trying to ignore the dragon's bait.

"In a sense," Jolsu growled.

"Is that what you're waiting for, then? To be alive?"

Jolsu's golden eyes fixed sharply on Zak. "Why do you care?"

"Well," Zak started, quickly piecing together what he knew. "It seems you've been trapped in every *Nacusti* in my bloodline, which is why you said you knew them all. So, you must be interested in continuing the line for a reason. Is it possible to reverse the ritual you performed with Adrastus?"

The dragon didn't move for what felt like an eternity, and his golden eyes seemed to peer directly through Zak. Finally, Jolsu broke the silence.

"I could be *more* alive, but none of you *Nacusti* would dare to sacrifice like your namesake. Like *I* did."

"How do you know? What if we haven't been given the chance?"

Jolsu's upper lip curled back, exposing his set of lethal teeth as a guttural noise escaped his throat. "How DARE you assume knowledge of MY life, of MY *Nacusti*! Do you think I haven't tried to live again? You think I *enjoy* being trapped in the heads of an endless line of bumbling mages?"

The dragon's head reared, and a jet of green fire erupted from his jaws, shooting into the sky and briefly illuminating the strange beach.

Zak jumped back. "I'm sorry!" he shouted to be heard above the blaze.

The flames stopped, and Jolsu's eyes snapped back to Zak.

"You ask more, and perhaps better, questions than your predecessors. Yet you overstep, *Parignis*."

Something felt different. Zak felt heavy suddenly; it was like his thoughts were slower, and his speech was more difficult.

"I..." Zak attempted.

"We've spoken long enough," Jolsu countered. "It seems you may be as useless as the rest. You're welcome, by the way, for saving your friend." Jolsu's eyes bored into Zak as he gave one last wicked smile, raised one of his front paws and pushed Zak backward.

Before Zak could ask what Jolsu meant, he felt a rush of air and a sudden falling sensation as everything faded into darkness.

CHAPTER 26

BENEVITA

Zak woke with a start, his chest heaving up and down.

"Easy now, you're safe," Bazil said. The priest had been sitting in a chair beside Zak's bed. Bazil stood, easing him back as his breathing slowed to a more relaxed pace.

As he gained his bearings, Zak looked around the room. Grey stone walls supported tall, vaulted ceilings. Beds lined the walls as white curtains hung around each, able to open and close for privacy. Stained glass windows divided the stone, depicting individuals in gold, silver, and lavender robes. Some stood tall, and others bent to help injured or sick figures. The light filtering through the glass cast myriad colors into the room, mixing into a bright, almost happy glow.

"Where are we? What happened?" Zak asked.

"We're in the Temple of Light, in the healing wards," Bazil answered calmly. "You've been here before, remember?" He gestured to the figures in the stained glass windows. "These are some of our exalted healers from the last few centuries."

"Where's Olivia?" Zak asked. He felt his breathing begin to quicken again.

"She's okay. She's in the ward across the hall." Bazil's expression was softer than usual, which worried Zak.

"How long have I been sleeping?" His tone sharpened, annoyed he constantly needed to ask questions.

"About two days," Sorwin said, walking to stand at the foot of Zak's bed. He entered the room without Zak noticing.

"What happened?" Zak asked Sorwin. "I don't remember anything after seeing Olivia on the ground."

"Much has happened, in short," Sorwin started. "Are you sure you're ready to...?" he trailed off, gesturing vaguely at the bed and the room, perhaps indicating his situation.

"Yes," Zak said, wincing a little as he adjusted to a sitting position. He felt tremendous pain in his arms, legs, and shoulders as he moved. Most of his body was bandaged again, presumably treating the aftereffect of his transformation. He took a deep breath to steady himself. "Yes, please, what happened?"

"Well, most importantly, everyone is alive," Sorwin said with the briefest of smiles. "Shira recovered quickly on the field and helped scout where we found you. Tansil will tell us more about her report, I think. Kaleb was in the bed next to you recovering and was released yesterday. The Druid, unfortunately, was captured by Renna, if you recall."

"Terasi," Zak said, nodding solemnly.

"Ah, I see you do." A moment passed in silence before Sorwin started again. "Our young Kalbick is just there," he gestured to Zak's right.

Two beds down, Zak saw Kal's head and the tops of his shoulders poking from beneath the white covers of the healing ward bed. He lay motionless except for the shallow rise and fall of his chest.

"He's bound in sleep until we can figure out what happened during his time with the Consortium and between the two of you."

Zak couldn't help but smile as he watched his friend, no more than twenty paces away. He looked peaceful as he slept.

We did it, he thought. *We saved Kal.*

"Could I see Olivia?" Zak asked. Knowing Kal was safe, he wanted to confirm Olivia's well-being with his own eyes.

Sorwin tilted his head toward Bazil inquisitively.

"If you can move well enough, yes, but I'm not sure she wants to see you." Bazil said flatly.

"What do you mean?" Zak asked, his eyes darting between Bazil and Sorwin.

"Perhaps it's best if you *do* see her to understand," Sorwin said quietly.

"Slowly," Bazil said with a sigh. He pulled back the blankets of Zak's bed and helped him stand.

As it turned out, Bazil didn't need to recommend a speed. Having been unconscious for several days, Zak moved slower than the elders in his village. He leaned heavily on the priest as every step sent a wave of pain up his bandaged legs. He was determined, though, to see Olivia.

Sorwin, walking ahead of the hobbling pair, pushed open the large wooden doors that sealed the healing ward. A twin set stood across the hall. With a gentle wave of his hand, the dark wood parted and closed behind them as they entered the room. It was nearly identical to the ward they had just left.

Olivia was propped upright in a bed at the end of the left side of the room. She leaned against a pile of pillows that supported her back and head as she stared out the window to her left.

As they walked closer, Zak saw her eyes were swollen and red and her complexion paler than usual. Still, he thought she had never looked more beautiful. Seeing her sitting in that bed, very much alive, was all he could have wanted. A scowl took residence on her face at the sight of Zak.

"How could you!" she said as Zak hobbled close to her, moving as quickly as he could with Bazil's help. He leaned in for a hug and awkwardly fell on her, squeezing her tight. He didn't plan to do this, but he was too happy to see her to contain himself. She was momentarily stunned. "Stop! What are you doing?" She pushed him away and winced with the effort.

"I'm just happy you're alive," he said, pulling himself upright. "'How could I' what?" he asked, confused.

"You *bound my magic*!" she hissed.

Zak stared at her blankly. His lack of understanding seemed to upset her more.

"Seriously? You ruined my life, and you have no idea what you did, do you?"

"It seems," Sorwin interjected, "You performed a *vitaligo*, a life binding, on Olivia."

"What does that mean?" Zak asked.

"It's an old magic," Bazil answered. "One that prevents

death but binds one's soul to their magic. It means if Olivia uses magic, she will drain her life force."

"No," Zak said. "No, I didn't do this, I couldn't! I don't know how..." he stammered as his mind spun in circles.

"Magic is about intention, *Nacusti*," Olivia spat. "Obviously, you don't know what you're doing, but it doesn't stop you from doing it."

Zak gasped. "Jolsu! It was Jolsu! That's what he meant; he said, 'You're welcome, for saving your friend.' Except he didn't seem to mean it."

"Who is Jolsu?" Bazil asked.

"The Guardian, the dragon that gave his power to Adrastus."

"You spoke with Jolsu?" Sorwin asked. His eyebrows raised, betraying his curiosity. Zak could tell he wanted to ask more questions, but with a look at Olivia, he seemed to think better of it at the moment.

"Briefly, yes. When I was unconscious. He's bitter and angry, but he needs me alive."

"Not all of us would agree," Olivia sneered.

"I'm sorry, Olivia, I had no idea," Zak said, turning to his once-friend. "If *Nacusti* magic did this to you, maybe it can undo it."

Olivia didn't respond but huffed as she drew the bed covers closer to her chest, turning as much as she could away from Zak and toward the window.

"That is a possibility," said a voice behind the group.

They all turned simultaneously as Tansil glided over to them. His dark yellow robe fluttered softly as he came to stand at the foot of Olivia's bed. The elf's bright green eyes lightened the glowing room even more.

"Really?" Zak asked, feeling his hope grow.

"In theory, yes. If something hasn't been done before, it doesn't mean it's impossible," Tansil answered.

Zak deflated a little, realizing the enormity of the task of reversing an ancient ritual.

"We'll discuss the finer points of Ms. Pratinos' predicament soon. For now, I'd like to apologize."

Zak and his friends all stood silent, unsure of what Tansil meant. Eventually, the elf realized there was some confusion.

"To all of you," he added.

"What for?" Zak asked, a little more blunt than he intended.

"I requested that Sorwin withhold information from you, Zakolor, about the *indagomius* and our plan until we were sure it would work. That led to the series of events that landed you all here after much danger and risk to your lives. For that, I'm deeply sorry."

There was complete silence for a few moments as it seemed no one knew what to say. Finally, Sorwin shifted his stance before he spoke.

"I know you had the best intentions for all of us, Archmagus. I wouldn't presume we blame you for any of this." His last statement was almost a question as he looked across the group. Zak and Bazil quickly shook their heads. Olivia said nothing and continued staring out the window.

"Regardless," Tansil continued. "My miscalculation is why we are here. Zandorn would never have been so reckless with an open confrontation in the past. Most of the continent doesn't even believe there *is* a war because of his secrecy. He operates in the shadows, leaving little evidence of his doings. Even though we know he's causing the decay of the very earth we stand on, we can't definitively prove that to the masses. Something is different, something has changed," explained the Archmagus.

"Zandorn left Tor'alan over a century ago. People do tend to change," Bazil observed.

"That is my point exactly; he hasn't changed in all that time. Until now, at least, with the rediscovery of the *Nacusti* line."

"What do you mean?" Zakolor questioned.

"In your grandfather's time, Zandorn didn't know he needed *Nacusti* blood for his experiments," Tansil said. "After Zandorn left and began antagonizing individuals with rare magics for his research, your grandfather went into hiding. He was, to his credit, overly cautious, and wanted nothing to do with Zandorn or those opposing him. At that time, it was mostly myself and the other magical houses. The League had yet to be formed."

"Yes, you told me this when I first arrived." Zakolor thought for a moment, recalling his first conversation with Tansil.

"It wasn't until a few years before your birth that Zandorn realized he needed divine magic. Your grandfather was gone, and your mother remained in hiding."

"You brought me to Tor'alan because you said it was safer than anywhere in the four kingdoms," Zak stated.

"Correct," Tansil answered.

"Why didn't my mother seek refuge here?"

The elf sighed deeply. "Along with great power, your family also carries great stubbornness. Your grandfather was firm in his beliefs to avoid this conflict. Your mother, Kamira, honored his wishes and did the same."

"You tricked Zakolor, then." Olivia finally spoke, settling an unnerving gaze on Tansil.

"In what way?" Sorwin asked.

"Did you tell him his family's choices? Their views on the war?"

"No, but we thought—"

"Exactly, *you* thought! You didn't let *him* think for himself! There seems to be a trend developing, *Magerus*." She spat the last word with venom.

"Olivia!" Bazil whispered fiercely. Even the stoic priest looked shocked at her words.

"What?" She turned on Bazil. "They lied to him, coddled him, and now look at what's happened! He bound my magic without even realizing it!"

"You're half right," Zak said steadily. The others fell silent and looked at him. "I should have been told more, educated more, about my powers. But what my family believed is irrelevant. They were wrong."

"Zak..." Olivia said.

"No, they were," he continued. "They had the power to change this war, to save countless lives. They chose to hide away and protect themselves instead. I won't do the same."

"If that is how you feel, I think there is someone you

should meet," Tansil said.

"Do you think he's ready?" Sorwin asked the Archmagus.

"I have to be," Zak answered, finding an unfamiliar strength in his voice.

Tansil nodded, perhaps approvingly. "I think you two should come as well. It may be...enlightening," he offered, indicating Olivia and Bazil.

It was Zak's turn to nod his agreement as he looked at Bazil and Olivia.

"Yes, well, you can't really get anywhere without me now," Bazil said, readjusting his grip on Zak's waist as he continued to support him.

Olivia sighed and threw back the blankets on her bed roughly, wincing despite herself. She stood and lifted the red and silver elementalist robe from a hook near her bed, quickly fitting her arms through it and pulling it closed.

Sorwin offered Olivia an arm, which she seemed to accept reluctantly. The hobbling pairs of Zak, Bazil, Olivia, and Sorwin were quite a sight as they followed Tansil through the halls of the Temple of Light, out the front door, and across the fresh, green lawns of the Center. A midday sun shone directly down on the floating city, passing clouds offering sparse relief from the light and heat. Despite his pain, Zak's muscles relaxed slightly in the sunlight, taking in the warmth.

"Thank you, Bazil," Zak said as they ambled on the cobblestone path behind Tansil, Olivia, and Sorwin.

"For what?" the priest asked, grunting as he supported nearly half of Zak's weight.

"For everything," Zak answered. "You kept most of us alive during that fight, especially Olivia. Thank you."

"I think your shield had something to do with the 'keeping us alive' bit. But you're welcome."

Due to their slow pace, the relatively short walk to the castle from the temple dragged on. Zak noticed many glances and subsequent whispers in his direction as various mages and soldiers passed through the Center.

"It seems rumors of our battle have spread rather quickly amongst the public despite the council's desire to keep it quiet," Bazil observed with a dry tone.

Zak swore he almost saw the priest smile, but he'd never tell Bazil, of course. He was too proud of his stoic reputation.

"What a shame," Zak said, echoing his friend's tone, appreciating their mutual dislike of the council. He wouldn't have been surprised to learn if Bazil was the one that started the rumors.

Once inside the castle, the group wound through many passageways and down many staircases. Several times along the way, Tansil had to wave down various guards, mages, and enchantments for the group to proceed safely. Wherever they were going and whoever they were meeting, there was no way Zak would have encountered them by chance.

Finally, they halted at a large door carved of both the lightest and darkest of stone. It depicted a battle between light and dark magics, one force emerging from either side, each struggling to overtake the other, but neither appearing as the victor. In the middle, where they met, a green circle illustrated the cyclical nature of life.

"Light and dark, while mutually exclusive, need the other to exist. They are the forces that pull at all forms of life," Tansil explained. "Behind this door, you will meet your past and future, Zak. We can follow you down this path, but you must forge the way. Are you prepared?"

"I am," he answered, his throat catching. He didn't feel he had a choice.

Tansil nodded, turned, and pressed both palms to the door. The stone carvings seemed to come alive, and the battle reversed. Figures that were intertwined disconnected, swords that crossed became uncrossed, and spells that clashed returned to their casters. The forces of light and dark retreated to the edges of the door frame, and as they did, the center green circle glowed brightly before filling the now empty spaces on the door.

As it glowed, Tansil lifted his hands, and the door opened with the loud grinding of stone on stone echoing in the hallway. They moved inside the room beyond the door.

It was ornate, with cascading murals, beautiful tapestries, and elaborate masonry work. Glistening arches supported by rows of carved pillars ran the room's length.

At the opposite end sat three giant, incredible thrones. On the left was a pure white throne, its angular features perfectly and expertly cut. On the right stood an obsidian-colored throne. This one was jagged and uneven, twisting along the top and base. It looked almost as if billowing smoke had solidified. In the middle was a green throne. At first, Zakolor thought it was carved, but as they neared the tall seat, he realized it was a living tree. Its branches wove a delicate but solid perch as the back stretched high, fanning out with beautiful leaves of varying colors.

They stopped a few paces away from the thrones. They were far too big for any human, elf, or creature he knew to fill them. Who sat in them? Who were they meeting?

"Sorwin, if you would, please," Tansil said in his clear, direct voice.

Sorwin nodded and gently lifted Olivia's arm from his, placing it gingerly on Bazil's side opposite Zak. Zak wondered what the stranger's first impression would be of them, with him and Olivia both supported by Bazil.

As he walked forward, Sorwin pulled a small leather pouch from a hidden pocket in his robe. It had a palm-sized gem inside with an impossible array of colors.

"What is that?" Zak asked, not sure if either Bazil or Olivia would know.

"It's called a *cordeus*," Olivia said. "It's the heart of a god."

"Why does Sorwin have one of those?" Bazil asked. "Don't the Archs usually carry them?"

"The Archs?" Zak interrupted.

"The Archmagus, Archlumen, and Archalium. They lead the magical houses," Bazil answered.

Zak was familiar with Tansil, of course, and Vermig and Sashina after his run-ins with the council, but he had never heard them collectively referred to as "the Archs."

Olivia shrugged. "For some reason, Tansil gave the *cordeus* to Sorwin. I never asked why."

Zak turned his attention back to Sorwin—a tiny hole formed in the twisting branches as he neared the center green throne. Sorwin carefully set the *cordeus* in the offered space, stepped back, and stood next to Tansil.

There was a bright flash of light, and Zak winced, shielding his eyes. After a moment, he blinked them open and saw a soft glow fill the room. In the center throne sat a beautiful, green-skinned woman. Her brown hair flowed elegantly down her shoulders to the throne's base. Her green, yellow, and brown garb glittered magnificently in the soft light emanating from her presence.

Zak and everyone else there with him was utterly stunned. His stomach leaped into his chest as he realized he must be looking at a god. For a long time, no one said anything as they stared at the incredible being before them. Eventually, Tansil broke the silence.

"*Benevita*, Mother," he said, taking a few steps forward and plunging into a low bow.

The woman tilted her head forward slowly, which Zak interpreted as her acknowledging Tansil. With this, the elf continued.

"I have brought the *Nacusti* to meet you, Mother. It is time he learned from your wisdom and embraced his potential." Tansil turned back to Zak with his arm extended, offering his hand.

Zak took a hesitant look at Tansil, then Bazil. He carefully unhooked himself from the priest and hobbled forward a few steps. He was surprised yet thankful his injured legs carried him.

Zak nodded his thanks to Tansil but did not take his offered hand. Even before she started speaking, Zak had the feeling he knew her, knew who she was. He wanted to meet her standing on his own.

"*Nacusti*," she began. Her voice resonated within him. It was as if she spoke through him, to his very essence. She looked down, her deep brown eyes staring into his face. "*I am Cerevita, Goddess of Life and Mother of Magic. We have much to discuss.*"

"We do," Zakolor agreed.

GLOSSARY AND PRONUNCIATIONS

CHARACTERS

Ageric Keldin (uh-jare-ick): Zakolor's father, blacksmith of Densba

Bazil Ben (bas-ill): priest in the League and Zakolor's friend

Bill Solura (bihl): Kalbick's father, blacksmith of Densba

Burvenin (burr-venn-in): Magerus, general of the Consortium

Clairise Keldin (clare-eese): Zakolor's mothery

Elpida (ell-pih-duh): bronze lizard, Terasi's companion

Euphemius Van Ilia (you-fem-ee-us): merchant, member of the League's council, Olivia's sponsor

Gunther (gun-thur): Renna's servant

Gyrnavo (gear-nah-voh): King of Weslinton

Jeppida Qor (jep-id-uh core): Prime Minister of the Republic of Evartia

Jolsu (jole-soo): dragon, Zakolor's guardian

Joryl (jore-ill): Densba council leader

Kalbick Solura (kal-bihk): Zakolor's best friend

Kaleb Deidaku (kay-luh day-dah-koo): major in the

League's army

Karazul (care-uh-zool): assassin working for Zandorn

Limba Dar (limb-buh): advisor to High King Marius

Lupa (loop-uh): general and leader of the League's army

Marius Fern (mare-ee-us): High King and leader of the League's council, King of Regadensia

Marralee Solura (mare-uh-lee): Kalbick's mother

Olivia Pratinos (oh-liv-ee-uh): elementalist in the League, Euphemius' ward, and Zakolor's friend

Renna (wren-uh): Zandorn's daughter

Sashina (sosh-in-uh): Archlumen, leader of the Temple of Light

Shira Motchit (sheer-uh): summoner in the League, Sorwin's friend

Sorwin Darlangson (soar-win): Prince of Darlangson, Magerus, Zakolor's magus

Tansil Windover (tan-zill): Archmagus, Magerus, leader of the House of Elements, elven

Terasi (teh-rah-see): Druid

Vermig (vir-miig): Archalium, leader of the Den of Darkness

Ymona (ee-mohn-uh): former Queen of Evartia

Zakolor Keldin (zak-oh-lore): Nacusti

Zandorn (zan-doorn): Magerus, leader of the Consortium

PLACES

Accipia: a village near Sorwin's castle that was a hideaway in his youth.

Bernadooth: largest port city in the Southern Isles, on the northern tip of Carshandyn.

Carshandyn: the largest of the Southern Isles, where Densba and Bernadooth are located.

Darlangson: western kingdom and member of the League. Home to Sorwin.

Densba: small village on the southern side of Carshandyn, where Zak is from.

Florinshire: a village on the plains of Darlangson, reportedly where Zak's true parents were hiding when he was born and they were killed by the Consortium.

Gort'haal: southwestern country and land of the dwarves. They were furious with the destruction of the Guardian War and soon after buried themselves in their mountain home. No dwarf has been seen since.

Lindomer: port city on the southern tip of Regadensia.

Nalawin: northern country and land of the elves. While a few stray elves interact with the outside world, the country closed its borders centuries ago, isolating itself from the rest of Valecium.

Pywell Mountains: hiding place of the Consortium, where Zandorn has found a way to survive in the Rot and extend lifespans beyond the mortal coil.

Regadensia: central kingdom and member of the League. Led by High King Marius Fern.

Republic of Evartia: eastern country and member of the League. Recently underwent a rebellion, overthrowing its previous twin monarchs and establishing a democratic republic. Led by Minister Jeppida Qor.

Tor'alan: capital of the League. The floating city usually resides near the middle of Regadensia.

Wastelands: formerly a country, the land was devastated as a result of the Guardian War.

Weslinton: eastern kingdom and member of the League. Led by King Gyrnavo.

MAGIC

Anima mea telum: appear, weapon of my soul

Aquatelum: water spear

Dormiligo: sleep binding

Dormio: sleep

Fumus: smoke

Ignis: fire

Relentesco: slow

Sylvaligo: wood binding

Tegoperignis: fire shield

Visus accipiter: sight of the hawk

Vitaligo: life binding

OTHER

Archalium: leader of the Den of Darkness. Vermig is the current title holder.

Archlumen: leader of the Temple of Light. Sashina is the current title holder.

Archmagus: leader of the House of Elements. Tansil is the current title holder.

Benevita: blessed life, an old-fashioned but still used greeting and parting phrase.

Cordeus: heart of a god, a powerful magic artifact.

Indagomius: a pair of charmed gems used for tracking magic.

Magerus: powerful mage that has mastered at least one discipline of magic and has considerable skill in several others

Nacusti: Guardian-born

Parignis: Little Fire

Stulmati: Evartian slang for idiot.

ACKNOWLEDGEMENTS

This is one of those pinch-me moments, something that doesn't quite feel real. It's an odd thing to have worked on this book for so long, in so many different moments of my life, and to finally have it done — or as done as it will most likely be.

I started writing Zakolor when I was eighteen and about to begin college. I've always had a vivid (read: overactive) imagination, and that imagination often manifested in daydreams. When those daydreams started having recurring characters, I decided to start capturing them, and that was the beginning of Zak's story. Now, just before I turn thirty-two, I'm finally publishing his journey.

Without my parents, Zak would not exist. Thank you for reading *Lord of the Rings* and *The Hobbit* to us before bedtime. It's an endeavor I can only marvel at now; the patience required to read Tolkien to seven- and eight-year-olds is astounding. It means the world to me, and I am confident that your perseverance sowed the seeds of Valecium.

Thank you to Papa, Christopher, and Paul for being the brave first readers. Your time and willingness to explore are more valuable than you know.

Thank you to Mama for your keen eye and attention to detail in editing.

To Alfredo, for listening to my ramblings for years. It isn't easy being my partner, let alone visualizing the world in my head. Thank you for your patience and understanding.

Lastly, thank you, Reader, for making it this far. Having this opportunity to share this world I've discovered is truly beyond my wildest dreams. I hope this is the first of many, many chances I have to introduce you to Valecium and the stories of the *Nacusti*.

Until next time. *Benevita!*

ABOUT THE AUTHOR

J. R. Douglas has been writing as a hobby since he was a teenager. While he keeps busy working in adult education, tending his garden, and trying to stay healthy with some yoga, he plans to continue sharing the world of Valecium through the Nacusti Chronicles. J. R. lives in upstate New York with his partner and their sweet dog, Samson.

www.ingramcontent.com/pod-product-compliance
Lightning Source LLC
Chambersburg PA
CBHW061428150726

47987CB00001B/130